The Thief of Secrets

Celma Ribeiro

bound to publish ≪

Produced by Bound to Publish
www.boundtopublish.com

ISBN-10: 0615841929
ISBN-13: 978-0615841922

for Elena

Once Upon A Time

My Lord,

forgive me for I have sinned. And Lord, forgive me for I have betrayed you in war and in peace. My blood will remain in this earth and my bones will turn into dust. And so, there will be the one who will be forgotten. Now Father, you may take me into your wings or into the confines of hell, for I, and only I know, the secret which will lay with me.

Chapter 1

Amsterdam, 1994

WHEN I WALKED THROUGH THE HEAVY, dark mahogany door, I swore it was going to be the last time I would see him. I was determined to get the business done and forget about it. It had caused too much agony and despair. I was still young and was going to erase it from my mind and start a new life.

It seems like I have tried to forget things and start a new life for a long time now.

But wait a minute . . .

In my mind, flashes of the painting I saw while walking on the streets of Amsterdam kept haunting me. It was all I could think about for the last hour. I remember every detail, color and feeling in that painting.

I had just left the famous Yellow Submarine Café.

"You can't go to Amsterdam and not go to the submarine," I remember Cristina and Agustín telling me the night we spent on their Grandpa's veranda overlooking the sea.

"It is a must," the Grandpa said from his rocking chair listening to our conversation. So, I decided to pay a visit to the coffee shop in honor of my dear friends, whose grandfather I will always remember.

I went in, ordered a cup of coffee and a slice of pie, while people around me were smoking the most exotic herbs from around the world. Nothing shocked me nor excited me by then, but I still smiled imagining Cristina and Agustín deciding on the herb menu on their trip to the submarine. I finished my coffee and my pie, paid my bill, and the café became part of my past.

The streets of Amsterdam were alive even though it was drizzling and the cold was burning faces and hands. It was the beginning of April, not summer yet, and it felt good to be all bundled up in some warm clothes—but not for long.

I was in Amsterdam because Roland had decided that I would be safe there—as if he gave a damn about my safety. I had time to spare before meeting him at the pub, so I lost myself to the streets for a few hours. And it was there, when I was walking on the *Spiegelstraat*, that a dim light grabbed my eyes. Down by my feet a glass window let the light shine through. I bent down and I saw it.

It was a small gallery in the basement of the old building standing by me. Inside, some paintings were hanging on the wall, some were on the floor; lying against old furniture and one painting was sitting on an easel. It was the most beautiful scene I had ever seen.

That painting carried me away to the middle of some sea. I felt as if I was standing on a ship looking at land. The land before me was green, and the water below was a nameless shade of blue that I can't properly describe. Tall, slender coconut trees were swaying in the wind and the light on the mountains was revealing all the crevices in the land.

The sand was white and deserted as if it was waiting for me to arrive.

I held my breath for a second and I came back to reality. I did not want to make him wait.

Chapter 2
Roland

SINCE I WAS A LITTLE GIRL I had dreamt of a beautiful tropical island, but nothing like the painting I saw in the small gallery. The scene in that painting surpassed all my dreams. I walked away from it because I did not want to be late for my meeting with Roland. Not that I couldn't wait to see him, but because I wanted to get the business done and forget about it.

I walked through the door and saw him sitting by the bar. My heart jumped. Only God knows how much I despised him.

"Hello Marina," he said, with his cold smile.

"Hi Roland," I answered, regretting having waited so long to face him.

He sized me up and took a long sip of his drink. Without saying a word he passed me the envelope and ordered my favorite beer.

It seems like Roland knows everything about me. More than I do at times. *But today I am the wise one. He doesn't know that this is the last time he will see me, and how much I hate him.*

We first met in the airport in Casablanca, Morocco. It was February of 1991.

I had come out of the airport bathroom talking to myself

and feeling humiliated because I had been given ten inches of toilet paper by a gentleman standing at the door of the lady's room—*ten inches of miserable paper, for me to do my business.*

"This is terrible isn't it?" Roland said, as I exited the room.

I raised my eyes from drying my hands on my clothes and gave him a halfhearted smile, agreeing with him.

"How about a drink while we wait for our flight?" he said grabbing my carry-on and walking towards the only coffee shop in the airport. Speechless, I followed him, because as he held my carry-on, my destiny was in his hands.

Chapter 3

Killing the Chicken, 1975

I GREW UP IN BRAZIL, a country full of flavor, love, and hate.

Full of flavor because of the diverse nationalities of which Brazil was made. Portuguese, Italian, Dutch and German had all come to the land in search of a brighter life.

Full of love; of course, because most of the people are Latinos, and we all know that Latinos are a race of open arms, hearts and hope. *Then, there is the hate, but that, I will tell you about later.*

Still, I could not imagine growing up anywhere else, since I believed that the flavor, and the love, made it all worth it.

My family was a typical Brazilian family.

Dad was the descendent of Portuguese immigrants who moved to Brazil leaving behind a fascist country.

Mom was a *Cabocla*—mixed by native Indio and Dutch immigrants; she was born with the exotic look that many Brazilians own.

They had me when they were young, and as we say in Brazil, "they put their rags together," and shared the same roof for a few years.

I don't remember much of those days, but I do remember mom packing us up and moving us to grandma's house.

Those were great days! Grandma's house became my fort.

I remember running up and down the dirt road where grandma's house sat. Shirtless, just wearing underwear and covered in red dirt from head to toe, I felt invincible. It was the happiest time of my life.

Sundays were always like a big party at the house. We all sat around the big old table in grandma's kitchen and savored the fresh chicken dish. I mean fresh, because a few hours prior to the feast, grandma would circle the poor thing and run in for the kill. One twist of the neck and the thing stopped clucking. It was terrifying, but at the same time exciting, to see how powerful my grandmother was.

Besides running up and down the dirt road with the kids of the neighborhood, my job was to make sure that the chicken that had been killed and boiled in hot water had no more feathers left on its skin.

So, every Sunday, I sat on the floor of grandma's veranda with the chicken in a big bowl, the bowl between my legs, and plucked the feathers off the poor thing. It wasn't a job I hated, but I much preferred to be running free, up and down the street, covering myself in dirt.

Like all good things in my life that came to an end, grandma had to die. With grandma there went the big old fort and the dirt road. There went the happy Sundays with the wretched chickens, and there went my childhood.

It was a bad thing having grandma die, because mom and I, we had to pack and move again.

Chapter 4

The Witches' Path, 1979

I WONDER WHAT MAKES PEOPLE do wondrous things in life. I wonder what it took for my ancestors to jump in a boat searching for a new world. The thing is, I will never know, since now, they are all buried under six feet of dirt. But I do know one thing; they must have had some gypsy blood in them, since I can't seem to stand on one piece of this earth for too long. In my life, there is always some packing to do, and new horizons to discover.

It all started when grandma died. As I said, it was a bad, bad thing. First, we had to move away from my fort, then, we had to move away from our city. The only condolence was that the place we were moving to was close to the sea.

I remember the morning the bus crossed our new town before making its stop at the central station. Sitting inside the bus, looking out the window, it was as if everything was passing in front of my curious eyes in slow motion.

The town's houses, they lined the cobblestone streets and their doors faced the road. The pastel colors which they were painted, gave them a distinct look under their clay rooftops. To me, it all looked surreal, since in those days, all I was accustomed to were my old surroundings—the ones like grandma's old fort, the dirt road where the fort sat facing the sunset, my old Catholic church, and the chickens. Oh yes, the chickens!

As I faced my new world from inside the bus, there was a strange feeling growing inside me. Back then, I could not recognize what it was, but now, after knowing what I know, I finally understand.

My new town was an old, old town, where many people had passed through it before me. Even he, in his glorious days, had visited its shores. Him, the man who would change my life.

Our new house was just like the ones I saw from inside the bus; door facing the road, a yellow pastel color splashed on the cement wall, sitting quiet under a clay rooftop. It was a nice place to be, and I started to feel strangely happy there, but what I soon found out fascinated me—we had moved next to the witches' house.

How excited I was. They, the witches, were the ones who peeked outside their windows as life passed by in front of their eyes and only God knows what went on inside their minds.

They, the seven sisters, who people believed to be witches, were used to people's amusement in them. They knew that it was the only way people could shield themselves, hiding behind the fear of knowing the truth. But I? I saw through their solitude. To me they looked wise, and it could possibly be that they were witches, and that they knew the future, which was in front of me. I have wondered at times if they could have advised me on things that were to come. Who knows if I would have chosen a different path.

It did not take much for me to make friends in our new town, and soon I felt as if I was home. Once we were settled, the witches' house became part of my daily route. No matter where I went, I made sure to place myself on the narrow sidewalk in front of their home. From there I could see them peeking at me while I waved to them, and, as always, there was no response on their part, not a wave, nor a smile, only their old grayish eyes approving of me.

I will never forget that time in my life. Then, I was still unaware of how my life would unfold and the future, which I was destined to live.

Those were days that I still had time to wander and wonder and so I did. I walked the old streets bordered by the sea and dreamed.

On the fishing boats, I could see the fishermen with their wrinkled faces—cigarettes drooping out one side of their mouths, sitting on their vessels, working on their nets. The boats, they seemed to patiently wait for the tide to moisten their keels, so they could wade again, and the men, they did not seem bothered by the waiting since they looked very content on their stranded ships.

My new home was a place where its saints sang above the church's bell, illuminating people's hearts. It was a marvelous place and I was happy to be there. The place will be in my memory forever, even now, as I swim in different seas. Still, I wish the witches had revealed my future to me.

Chapter 5

Morocco, 1991

AND NOW, HERE I AM, in this fucking airport, where everywhere I look, men are holding hands with big smiles on their faces, as if telling me that life is just perfect. And this stranger, whom I have never seen in my life, is carrying my carry-on. What was I thinking? Why did I let go of it? Fucking bathroom, in a fucking third world country, without a fucking paper towel for me to dry my hands. That was it! I put it down to dry my hands. How could I have been so stupid?

Just go along with the guy my mind kept telling me, *and get the carry-on back. That's all I have to do.* But my body was starting to sweat. It was the same cold sweats I had while laying in bed in the hotel room in Brazil.

 Rio de Janeiro, two days before

I could see the lights of the police car vanishing as I searched for it through my rear view mirror. I turned into the garage of the Copacabana hotel, turned the car's lights off, and rested my head on the seat's headrest. I sat there for a long time not believing what I had done. The chase was over. *Now,*

Douglas is probably proud of me, as he waits midway in Hell, for the truth to be told.

I got out of the car and crossed the dark garage of the hotel. As I entered the elevator, I could feel my body starting to fail. I opened the door of the room, threw the bleached blonde wig off my head and let my body fall on the bed. When I woke up, the chills had taken over me, and I was still feeling the anxiety of being chased, but I rested when I realized that it was already morning and that I was safe.

I knew I was safe because no one had noticed me leaving or coming back to the hotel, but then a feeling of guilt started to corrode my Catholic self. I had told a lie back at the monastery. Father Timóteo had been pleased that a young woman like me had chosen a life of chastity. *How could I have lied to such a nice priest?* He had personally shown me the way to the room where I found it, and after hours of digging through the old relics inside the walls of the monastery, it was finally in my hands. It was much easier than I thought it would be. Just like Douglas said: "They will let you in."

Back in Morocco, 1991

As I walked next to the stranger who had hold of my carry-on, all I could think was, *I must get it back. Concentrate Marina. Please don't lose it. Not now that you are so close to putting an end to it, and freeing the souls that are hanging around in Hell. You are the only one capable of setting them free.*

Don't lose now, I kept telling myself, and went along with the stranger who managed to have possession of the most valuable thing I owned. *Yes I own it! After six years. Now the search is finished and I must put an end to it.*

Chapter 6

Sunshine, 1983

I WAS SIXTEEN YEARS OLD when I got the job at the Pacific Bakery, back in the historic port town where I lived by the witches. It was a long time ago, but seems like it was just yesterday. I can still see it vividly every time I think about it. It was there, behind the bakery's counter, that I saw Douglas for the first time.

He was tall; he spoke with an accent, and wore reading glasses as thick as beer bottles. He came in, smiled and said, "Good morning Sunshine!" and that's when the world seemed to stop for me for the first time. He ordered and walked away with the smile still on his face and a baguette under his arm.

How excited I was. He called me Sunshine. Nobody had ever called me that before. So, there I was, sweet sixteen and swept off my feet by the charming old sailor.

I wondered where he came from and if he was staying, but all I knew about him was that he belonged to one of the ships that came to our waters now and then. He was different from all the sailors whom I had seen strolling down our old streets. He looked fearless. It seemed to me that he knew something that the rest of the world didn't know, for no one; no one had ever walked with such entitlement on those stones before. He fascinated me, and everyday, as he walked out of the bakery with the smile on his face and the baguette under his arm, I watched him strut down the cobblestone road as if he owned it.

One night, I dreamed about him. I dreamed of a fire, fire and rain. I dreamed that I was burning in hell, when he came to save me sailing in his boat. When I woke up the next morning I vowed to forget about him. What was I thinking? I was becoming fixated on a man I didn't know. I was making him into a hero—the hero of a story I hadn't lived.

I tried. I tried but it didn't work, and I knew it was dangerous to be feeling the way I felt toward a stranger, but I couldn't help it—the emotion inside me was consuming my soul.

So it continued that the highlight of my day was when his statuesque self would enter the bakery's door and greet me with "Sunshine." That kept me dreaming, that kept me wondering.

I wondered about what he knew and the places he had been. I wanted to know, I wanted him to tell me all about it, but I never asked.

Sadly the "Sunshine" didn't last and one day it was gone. On the wind his sail unfurled and away from our shores his ship drifted. He was gone. Gone from my sight, and gone from my heart. Just like that. I would never see him again—not on those shores.

—————————————————— Back in Morocco, 1991 ———

Now, the stranger carrying my carry-on in the airport at Casablanca, walking with the same entitlement as Douglas had when I was a teen, was making me feel sick to my stomach.

If he only knew what he was carrying . . .

Chapter 7

Flight 804 to Lisbon, 1991

IT SEEMS LIKE IT WAS ONLY YESTERDAY that I was a happy child, contemplating life, back at the bakery's counter. It was just yesterday that I marveled at the future ahead of me. But that was a long time ago, when I was young and innocent—a dreamer, if you will allow me to say.

I'm not a child anymore and I'm trying to forget the past and the dreams, but there's no time now because I have to get rid of this guy, who is still holding my carry-on.

"Yes, I'm on my way to Lisbon," I said, trying to sound casual, sitting next to him at the airport café. "And you?" I asked trying little to be polite.

"Portugal too, I can't wait to get there," he said, ordering us coffee.

I had not finished drinking my coffee yet, when he grabbed my carry-on again, which I had managed to put between my legs, and demanded, "Let's go, our flight is starting to board."

That's when I heard, "Flight 804 to Lisbon, departing from gate seven. All passengers please proceed to check in."

I walked next to him without taking my eyes off my carry-on, and feeling strange in my own skin. All I could think was *"Don't lose the bag, don't lose the guy. Don't lose the guy. Get my . . . back, get it back, back . . .* " It was then, that I remembered another man who had had the same effect on me that the stranger was having. It was seven years ago.

Back at the place, where the saints
─────────────────── sang above the church's bell ───────

"Do not follow the guy, don't go up these stairs, do not lie by him, don't let him do this to you . . . " my young and starving soul was yelling at me, but reason had vanished. I was only seventeen.

I was still living there, in the port town, walking the beach and wondering, when I got my foot caught between the rocks in front of his house.

He was there, by accident.

I saw him coming down the stairs to rescue me from my clumsiness, and my heart skipped a beat.

There he stood, without any precaution, in front of me asking, how did I manage to get myself stuck between the rocks.

His blue eyes were almost like aquamarine—a jewel. His dark blond hair looked like it had never seen a brush. The little tangles here and there gave him some attitude, or perhaps it was his attitude that made his tangles acceptable. The tan of his skin was not one of someone who lay for hours in the sun, but one, which the sun had chased. He walked towards me and as he tried to ease the rock holding my foot, he held my hand.

I thanked him for helping, and felt my face blushing with embarrassment. First, I had made a fool of myself by falling between the rocks. Then, I could barely stand on my own, so he had to continue holding my hand.

———————————————————————— Back in Morocco, 1991 ————

I did not lose my cool then, when I was seventeen, and now I can't lose it again, since the guy walking next to me in this fucking airport, is making me very uncomfortable.

Chapter 8

Upgrading

ROLAND'S STEPS WERE FIRM and precise, as if he had walked across those floors for an eternity. I let him walk ahead of me, and that's when I paid attention to him. He walked with an easiness that made me unsure of myself, and the more I noticed his ease, the more I wanted to lose him.

He was tall, slender, and his dark brown hair was perfectly cut and clean. The harsh jaw line on his face was broken by a cold smile, and his fierce hazel eyes told me not to trust him. I knew his suit was expensive, because of the way it hung on his shoulders—it let his body move freely and showed me the definition of his toned silhouette. But what distracted me the most were his hands. The precision with which they moved when he spoke was hypnotic, as if there was no need for words, and without any caution, I was following him, the stranger who was carrying my fate in his hands.

I was still following him as he arrived at the check-in area and walked to the first class counter, placing my carry-on by his feet. I stood next to him, and trying to reach for my carry-on, I said, "I have to go now. I'm flying coach," and I gave him a tired smile.

As if he had not heard what I said, he swept my ticket

from my hand, and gave it to the check-in clerk, telling her to "Upgrade Miss Marina's ticket."

Astonished, I tried to stop him. "Thank you, but I can't let you do this."

"Done already," was his curt reply.

My heart started to race and I felt dizzy. As I leaned on the airline's counter my arm touched his, making me feel worse. I took a deep breath, then another. "Roland, it is such a short flight," I said, trying to convince him.

Without answering, he handed me my upgraded ticket, grabbed my carry-on again and continued walking knowing that I was going to follow him.

I followed him to the gate, where the airplane was parked outside on the runway, and as we walked out of the building the fresh wind on my face made me feel better, but while we were climbing the stairs leading to the airplane, my life started to fast-forward in front of my eyes.

What is happening?

Where am I going?

My reverie was broken when he said, "Come on, we have to go."

He walked in front of me onto the airplane and I noticed his body becoming tense. Unaware of my own self, I noticed his eyes scanning the plane as if looking for something or someone, but after a few seconds his jaw eased, and his face relaxed.

"Soon we'll be home," he said, and continued walking to our seats.

I could not believe I was letting him lead me to my destination, and unsuccessfully, I tried to forget the reason why I was there, and appreciate the stranger who was kindly helping me.

The plane was half empty, but we still sat next to each other, and as we headed down the runway I was glad I was sitting, because when Roland took my hand and told me his secret, my knees failed.

"I don't like flying," he confided in my ear.

I tried to think of a response but nothing came out of my lips. They were numb. I was paralyzed. I wanted Roland to hold my hand forever; for the last time someone held my hand was a long time ago.

Chapter 9

Back Where the Saints Sang Over the Church's Bell, 1984

AFTER LUCIEN HELPED ME free my foot from between the rocks, he continued holding my hand as we walked up the stairs leading to his home. He said that I was "lucky" he had come to shore, leaving his boat anchored at the bay.

"What would have happened to you if I hadn't been here?" he asked me sounding intrigued.

I smiled, and didn't answer.

I had walked on that beach almost every day since Douglas' boat had sailed away, and never thought of any danger.

"I got here last night," he said while disinfecting the scrapes on my foot, which was making me quiver. "I was supposed to be in Curitiba today, but I guess it is a good thing I didn't leave, otherwise you would still be stuck on those rocks," he teased me, and carefully finished bandaging my scrapes and told me to stay away from the water for a couple of days.

Although I had just met Lucien, it was easy to be with him. He told me about his sailing trips up and down the coast of Brazil, and told me that he preferred life at sea. He said that he did not like going to the big city, and that he was only going because of his father's request.

"That's why I am here," he said, as if proving how lucky I was.

Even though he made me feel safe and relaxed, my conscience was telling me that I should not be alone in the house with the stranger. I had seen the house from the beach many times as I walked in front of it on my way to the rocks, but had never seen anyone around. It was always closed, and I remember thinking what a waste it was for such a nice place to be empty.

We talked as he put the bandages away in the medicine cabinet and I told him that I lived down by the market place. I told him that I wasn't from there, but since we had moved to the bay, I could not imagine living away from the sea. His sincere smile showed that he agreed with me.

He offered me a glass of water and we walked outside to see the colorful clouds touch the sea as the last light of the day played tricks with our eyes. We sat on the veranda of the big, white brick house, and I could see the rocks where I had sat many days watching the sunset. I did not know that those rocks could deceive you, as I had just found out.

Lucien and I sat there in silence, listening to the sounds of the waves as the stars started to glitter in the sky. It was springtime, and there was no traffic on the street other than a few lazy cars passing by.

Our silence was interrupted when Lucien told me that it was beautiful to see the land from the ocean. "Every time I enter a small bay it is like a new discovery. The people, the places . . . I love it," he said with starry eyes. "I'm planning a trip around the world," he told me, not taking a breath between words. "I want to see everything," he said, and as if daring me, he asked if I wanted to come with him.

"Yes, I would love to, but I don't think I can be in a boat without seeing land for too long." I said, and then, making fun of myself, I confessed that the only boat I had been on was one of the little dinghies by the bay.

He laughed, and said that it was all right.

"Next time," he said, and we kept watching the horizon.

Even though I knew he was just playing, I couldn't help but imagine being on a boat, sailing around the world.

I took a deep breath, a sip of my water, and daring myself I told him, "You know . . . I would love to travel the world too." I trusted him with my dream. "Maybe one day," I said with doubt, because I knew it was almost impossible.

He reached for my hand and we sat there looking at the ocean. His body next to mine made me feel uneasy, but as his skin gently touched mine, I did not move away.

That night, lying on the verandas' daybed, still watching the stars, Lucien whispered in my ears, "When you want something you have to go get it. You may not have it at first, but when you do get it, it will feel incredibly satisfying."

I closed my eyes and he hugged me tight.

"Follow your heart and don't give up when a door closes on you, there will always be another one to knock on."

I like to remember his words. It gives me hope. It makes me dream.

The summer I visited the witches on my search for Douglas, I drove past the home where Lucien told me such things, and I saw a beautiful family playing in the yard. The man holding the child made me smile. My heart felt warm, and then, in slow motion, I saw that it was Lucien. He looked deep into my eyes, all the way into my soul. How did he know it was me? The Alfa Romeo had tinted windows and my eyes were hiding behind my Ray-Bans. The bleached blond wig made me almost unrecognizable. I was hiding, but not from him. He knew. As the scene was moving away, I saw him smiling, watching me, until I was gone. It was our end.

Chapter 10

Hate

NOW, SITTING NEXT TO ROLAND, as he held my hand tight my heart was racing. *How does he know where I'm going?* I asked myself. *Where is my carry-on?*

I relaxed when I remembered him putting it in the luggage compartment above us. Still, with him holding my hand I drifted away.

I woke up when the airplane touched the ground in Lisbon and his hand was still attached to mine. I smiled at him trying to remember if I knew the stranger sitting next to me. No. I did not know him. I wondered if it was even real or if I was dreaming. After all, all I had lived through in the last few days, *I may as well be sleeping.*

As he let go of my hand a feeling of emptiness ran through my body. It had been a long time since anyone held my hand.

I let go of many things in my life. I let go of my family, I let go of my witches, and I left behind the peaceful white sand beach where I walked in the afternoons dreaming of horizons I wanted to discover.

But the sounds of the bullets still rang in my ears.

It was late night when I came home from spending the evening with Lucien. Feeling guilty but excited, I walked the long driveway leading to our front door and went inside to wash him off my skin. I found the house empty and I wondered where Mom could be.

I had just finished my shower, and was drying myself, when I heard footsteps outside the house. I remember thinking that it was Mom coming back home. I rushed to the entry door to let her in, but as I opened the curtain to the outside yard, what I saw made me tremble.

Outside our modest house, a man holding a gun was looking for a way to break in.

Terrified, I threw myself on the floor of our living room and crawled my way through the hallway, to where Mom's bedroom was. Once I made it into the room, I got inside the free-standing closet where I could hardly breathe, and sat on its floor. From there, I still could hear the footsteps moving back and fourth around the house.

We had no telephone. So, there I was, inside the closet, afraid I was going to die, and could not call for help.

I sat squeezed in that closet for what seemed like an eternity. I was terrified. I could not breathe, and was having difficulty concentrating and thinking clearly. All black. It was all the same with my eyes open or shut. I remember hugging myself against the clothes and blankets, and that's when I realized that Grandma's old rifle, which Mom had inherited, was hidden under the blankets.

"It is ok, shhh, I think he is gone," I thought, and carefully walked out of the stuffy box and crawled back to the living room. That's when I heard the explosion. One shot. I stood up and looked out the window. I saw Mom falling on the driveway. I pointed the rifle at the man, who now looked at me with horrified eyes, and I pulled the trigger. Time slowed. The sound of the bullets flying from the barrel terrified me, and I finally started to cry. One more bullet, one more . . .

And then there was silence.

No more bullets! No more footsteps. Everything became still. Only the thump in my heart and the salt on my lips made me realize I was alive.

Shhh, its ok . . . shhh.

The sound of the sirens brought me out of my trance, and that's when I understood what had happened. My heart raced in my chest as I hugged myself tighter. An eternity had passed since the sirens arrived and now there were footsteps inside the house.

I can't breathe.

The rifle was still in my hand and the footsteps were getting closer.

"Hello?"

The voice called again . . . "Hello?"

I opened the closet door slowly, where I had crawled back into, and the light shot in to my eyes.

I saw a witch.

She gently held my hand as she helped me out of the closet. She hugged me, and she touched my face. Her hand felt like ice on my burning skin. She asked me if I was all right.

I was crying. I could not stop crying.

"Your mother has been shot," she said. "She is on the way to the *Santa Casa*."

I knew it.

Emptiness took over my soul. It felt as if I had never lived before that moment. There was nothing left. Nothing.

Finally, I learned about the hate.

——————————— Back on the flight to Lisbon ———

And now, as the plane touches down, I have to let go of this stranger whose hand is comforting my disturbed soul.

Chapter 11

A Phone Call, 1991

As ROLAND RANG THE BELL by the door of the apartment where he was taking me, I heard footsteps hurrying our way. A charming white haired lady, perfectly coiffed and dressed, opened the door to us. She had a smile on her face and her eyes were brilliant with contentment. Looking at the nice heels on her feet, I could not help but think that she was probably in her seventies and that she looked darling for her age.

Roland hugged her and floated her in the air, kissing her cheek. He perfectly placed her back on the ground, where she blushed. She arranged her hair, which was still perfect, and patted down her skirt as she looked at me with curious eyes.

"One day he will give me a heart attack," she told me, as her cheeks got pink.

Feeling like an intruder, I smiled and kissed her cheek introducing myself.

"I am sorry for the inconvenience Miss Mary, but Roland insisted that I come," I told her, still shocked by the affection I had just witnessed between them.

"Who can say no to him, right?" she asked me holding my hands and looking me straight in the eyes.

"There is no way we would let her stay at the Ritz, would we Mary?" Roland asked her, and winked at me letting me know that he had an alibi.

"No. How could we do that?" Mary agreed.

"Come in honey, let me help you."

The apartment sat in an old building in Lisbon. The décor was comfortable and charming. Fresh flowers brightened the dining room table, while the crystal chandelier above it illuminated the room with a soft light. The flowery sofa across from the fireplace was so inviting that I felt like a kid, I wanted to go and jump on it. Everything in the place looked like it had been sitting comfortably for a long time; they were familiar with it. It was perfect, and Mary was perfect in her heels.

I followed her to the guestroom as the phone rang and Roland answered it. Between the few words he was saying to the person on the other end of the line, I heard, "Yes, we just arrived, she is here."

Did he really say "we"? I must be tired, hearing things, I thought.

Mary was the perfect hostess. She showed me the guestroom and started a bath for me.

"Never mind dressing up darling." she said, as she showed me the room. "And please make yourself at home," she told me, opening the bathroom window just enough so the fresh air could blow through. "I am going to prepare supper," she said, and left me to the quiet room.

I undressed and lay in the tub. The warm water almost put me to sleep. If it weren't for the magnificent cathedral stained glass window and the amazing view, I would have drifted off. It was marvelous.

I got out of the tub, dried myself with the fluffy towel Mary had given me and looked out the window at the rest of the view. Lisbon was still the same. Its old streets and buildings were beginning to feel familiar to me. There I felt safe. There I felt an accomplice to it. I knew her secrets and Lisbon knew my crimes.

I brushed my hair and tied it in a bun. I put on a comfortable dress and a bit of lip-gloss.

As I walked into the dining room I saw that Roland was still talking on the phone.

Is it the same phone call? I wondered.

He said goodbye to the person on the other end of the line and hung up the phone.

He stared at me for a while, which made me feel vulnerable. Until then he had been a perfect stranger.

He was still in the same clothes, but now his suit jacket was off and he was barefoot. The white wrinkled shirt with rolled up sleeves gave him a softer look, and I tried to pull my attention away from him, not wanting to jeopardize my plans.

I could hear Mary in the kitchen so I walked in and offered my help.

"Yes darling," she answered me. "Go sit by Land and get every bit of information you can out of him," she said in a playful tone, loud enough so Roland could hear. I had no choice but to do what she said.

I went back into the living room, and sat on the chair across from the sofa—which I still wanted to jump on. I couldn't, because Roland was sitting there, looking very much at home.

"Thank you for inviting me to stay," I said sincerely.

"Thank you," he said, sounding real.

"Mary loves having company. When I called her and asked her if I could bring you home she demanded that I do so," he said from the comfortable sofa.

He called her?

He asked her if he could bring me home?

My mind started to race again.

When did he call? We have been together since my humiliating bathroom experience at the airport in Casablanca.

He made no phone calls.

As my mind was troubling me, Mary walked in the room with a silver tray in hand, holding a decanter half-full with wine and two wine glasses.

"Here honey, try some of the best wine on earth," and she winked at Roland as she placed the tray on the table which was separating Roland from me. She poured us some of the burgundy liquid and walked away.

Dinner was stuffed squid, white rice and steamed vegetables, but first, she served us a traditional green bean soup that went perfectly with the delicious dinner.

"I made fresh chocolate mousse, Land, honey," she informed him coming back from the kitchen. In a second, he was on his feet again and kissing her cheek. Again she blushed. She loved him. She had raised him since he was a child when his mother had abandoned him to chase after some guy from France—Roland had told me that much while we were savoring the wine before dinner.

The apartment's intercom rang and Roland excused himself from the table to answer it. He came back to the dining room and told us that he was going to step out for a moment.

"It won't take long," he said, rushing to the door. I could not help but wonder where he was going.

Chapter 12

Risking

ROLAND DID NOT COME BACK when he said he would, just like my mother did not come back from the *Santa Casa,* the night she was killed.

Mary and I finished our dinner and I helped her clean up the table, while she told me stories of Roland growing up. There were so many of them that she wanted to share with me. It was late and I was exhausted, but she was so cheerful, talking about her Land, that I refrained from leaving her and going to my room.

"I always told him to call me grandma," she rolled her eyes, "but he insists in calling me Mary," she said proudly. "He says I don't look like a grandma. Isn't he darling?" She asked me, waiting for me to agree.

"My Land is very special, you know?" she continued, trusting me with her feelings. "I wonder who will be the lucky lady who will catch him." She said melancholic. "But to tell you the truth, I don't think he even wants one. He just doesn't seem interested. He is too busy with his work," she said with sad eyes. "I like having him around, but when I leave, I want him to have someone to take care of him. He needs to be taken care of, even though he doesn't show it."

What is happening to me? How did I end up in this kitchen listening to stories of Roland growing up? Eight hours ago he was a complete stranger who I wanted to tell to take a hike.

I can't think straight. I need some sleep.

I kissed Mary good night and excused myself to the guestroom where I found my luggage empty on the floor. Mary had hung all my clothes in the closet, except for my one black dress with the tiny sequins, which Mom had embroidered years ago. It lay on a chair next to the bed and reminded me that it was the only thing I never left behind. I marveled at the dress for a moment, and it reminded me of the innocent girl I once was and how much my mother had loved me.

I went to the bathroom, washed my face with the cool water and brushed my teeth. I let my hair fall down my back, and then I saw my face in the mirror and wanted to cry. I barely recognized myself.

What have I done?

I walked back to the room and dropped on the bed. My burgundy carry-on was sitting on the floor next to me. I thought about opening it and reading the letter, but the exhaustion had taken over my body and all I could do was lay in bed.

All right, I thought, and closed my eyes. That's when the events of the last few days raced through my mind in fast forward motion. I realized then that my ankle was still hurting from twisting it while running through the grass field, on my way to the Florianópolis bus station. It was there, back on the Island of Florianópolis, that I made the decision that led me back to Lisbon. I had decided that I was going to steal it. I was going to put an end to it and forget about it.

Yes Douglas, it is time.

If only it had been that simple.

Chapter 13

The Lady With Golden Hair, 1991

———————————— Three days before meeting Roland ————

THE TAXI DRIVER WHO WAS TAKING ME to the bus station told me that it would take a while to get there since renovations were being made on the bridge connecting the Island of Florianópolis, to mainland Brazil. Traffic was heavy; the taxi was barely moving, and I could see the station on the other side of the green grass field. To get there in the taxi would take too long. *I am going to miss the bus,* I thought, and decided to make a move. I paid the driver and got out of the car. All I had with me was a small backpack and my carry-on.

I was running towards the station when I saw a family of gypsies sitting under a tree, and that's when I missed a step and twisted my ankle.

The lady, who was the mother of the beautiful children sitting by her side, stood up and waved at me. I looked into her eyes with uncertainty, and then I looked behind me. *Maybe she is waving at someone else,* I tried to lie to myself. *No. Nobody behind me, and now she is coming closer.* I stood there and waited for her, and only now I do understand why I did it. She was the one who told me my fortune.

The beautiful smile she was carrying on her face showed me a perfect set of teeth. Her long golden hair, flowing down her back as she approached me, made her look surreal.

"No!" I told her, from behind my nervous smile, because I did not want her to get any closer.

I started to walk away from her when she grabbed my hand.

"Please," she said. "It will only take a minute."

"No, I have to go," I said reluctantly, trying to free my hand from hers.

"The bus will wait for you," she said, "but that is not what I want to tell you," she continued. "You are going to cross the ocean again on some big wings," she said and waited for my reaction.

"*What*?" I stopped and looked in her eyes. I was shocked by her revelation.

"Ok," I said, giving in and not resisting anymore.

Holding my hand she said to me, "Show me the biggest bill you have in your wallet."

Shit! I knew it. *There is always a catch.* I was in big trouble. *There is no way I'm giving my money to this woman,* I thought. But . . . how did she know? How did she know I was going to fly over the ocean?

"No," I said, and she freed my hand and I started to walk away from her.

"But you must know, don't you?" she insisted walking next to me. "How will I tell you your future, if you are not giving me anything in exchange?" she argued. "Nothing comes free," she concluded.

I opened my wallet and gave her my biggest bill. Now, my body was alert. She was making me uncomfortable.

Does she know me?

I was sure I had never seen her in my life, but my conscience was troubling me, and looking at her children under the tree, I walked away.

"Next time," I said, because I did not really want to know the future.

"No, Now!" she insisted following me.

What is her problem? She already got my money.

"You are not going to miss the bus," she said, and just like that, she grabbed my hand again and I finally gave in. With my hand in hers, she smiled, and she told me my fortune.

It took less than a minute and soon she was gone, back under the tree with her children, as if she had never touched my life. I ran as fast as I could, sure that I had missed the bus.

The midday bus departing to Rio de Janeiro was supposed to have left ten minutes ago. *What an idiot, letting myself be taken in by the gypsy.* I lost my money, and now *I am going to miss the bus.*

I made my way through the crowded station and walked on to the platform. There it was, just like she said—as if it was waiting, just for me. The driver standing by the door waved me in.

"Come on Miss, we are already late."

I sat down and felt the sweat dripping from my face. Her voice was whispering in my ear, "The bus will wait for you."

How did she know?

As the bus took me away from the station and the green grass field, where the gypsies sat under the tree, I held my carry-on tight and closed my eyes. A couple of hours to Rio, steal the dammed thing, and cross the ocean to Casablanca.

Chapter 14

Get Out

I WAS STILL AWAKE IN BED when I heard the entry door closing and footsteps vanishing at the end of the hallway. I remember thinking that it was Roland coming back. I drifted asleep and when I woke up the next morning the apartment was empty. I looked around it and I did not hear or see anyone.

Where are they?

I walked into the kitchen, and a jug of coffee sat on the table. A basket filled with bread and pastries was next to it. All of a sudden I realized how hungry I was. There was a note, which told me to make myself at home, and it was signed by Mary.

Where is Roland?

I felt as if I had woken up from a dream.

I have to get out of here, I thought.

I grabbed one of the pastries and shoved it in my mouth. Now that I was rested and awake, I realized what a fool I had been for letting a stranger take me to his home. I could not jeopardize my plans. I had everything figured out. I had to get out of there and fast. I poured a cup of black coffee and washed down the sweet pastry in my mouth with it. In my mind there was a voice telling me to run.

I went to the bedroom and packed my things—not forget-

ting my black dress. I brushed my teeth and tied my hair in
a bun. My carry-on was still sitting on the floor next to the
bed. I was putting my jeans on when I heard the front door
opening and someone walking in. My heart started to race
and I started to sweat. I looked around the room scanning for
anything left. No, everything was packed. Slowly I walked
from the room searching for either Roland or Mary, but was
surprised to see someone else.

"Good morning Miss Marina," said the tiny lady who was
looking busy in the kitchen.

"Did you sleep well?" She asked me, revealing a yellowing
smile on her wrinkled face.

"Good morning . . . " I said not sure if I had met her the
night before. "Yes, I slept well," and I smiled back at her.

The lady was busy, cleaning the few dishes in the sink,
when she told me, "Miss Mary said that when they checked
on you this morning, you were sound asleep."

*Did they really walk in the room while I was sleeping? What
nerve,* I thought. *Marina, you are risking all the work you have
done,* said the voice inside my head.

"What time are they coming back Miss . . . ?"

"Mena. My name is Mena," she told me, and kept busy at
the sink.

"Usually the lunch at the harbor doesn't end until three,"
she said looking at the wall clock, and that's when I realized it
was two in the afternoon.

"Oh my God! Did I sleep this much?

I tried to think fast but little Miss Mena kept on talking.

"I've been working for Miss Mary for more than thirty years," she informed me. "I've seen her lose her daughter and her husband, but she's still strong," the woman said, as if letting me in on a secret. "Of course, she has our Land," she muttered, and she poured me another cup of coffee. "He will never leave her, you know?" she told me looking at me with warning eyes.

"If it wasn't for his job, I don't think he would leave her at all," she continued. "But you know, he loves his job. He lives for his job and his grandma. Every time he has to leave town on his trips he makes sure to contact her. I wish my children were like that." And she looked away so I would not see the sorrow in her eyes.

Oh my God. What is happening? Who is this lady and why is she telling me all this?

"You know," she started again. "His grandfather was the Harbor Pilot here in Lisbon. Mr. Manuel took little Land to the port all the time, and Miss Mary—poor thing, she would worry until she saw little Land come running inside the house, telling her all about his day. Only then would she rest."

Why am I here listening to all this nonsense? Run Marina, Run.

Still, I could not leave Miss Mena without listening to her. She needed to share her stories with me. I felt as if she was telling me Roland's darkest secret, and for a moment, I pictured him as a little boy excited about his day.

I was heading for the hallway to go back to my room when she stopped me.

"She loves that boy, you know?" she said as if I should have known. "Poor Miss Mary, she never forgave her daughter for leaving little Land behind. When Sara left to go live with the French Mr., Miss Mary cried in bed for days. It was such a pity to see her in so much grief. But little Land? He knew what had happened and he never said a word. Even small like that, he had his ways set already, and when Mr. Manuel died, he became the man of the house. He's seen what a good man his grandpa was. Now, Land is as good as Mr. Manuel." The woman said proudly. "Lucky the one who catches him, but you know what, Miss? Miss Mary and I, we talk about it and we don't think there will ever be one. Our Land, he is too special."

Stop! My brain was screaming inside my head. *What's wrong with these people?*

No. I don't know Land. I don't want to know all this, and I don't want to be here. I need to get away, but she wouldn't stop talking.

Miss Mena walked to the dining room still muttering about how nice her Land boy was. *Now,* I thought. *I have to leave now.* I ran to the bedroom and closed the door behind me. I stood with my back against it, listening for any noise. There was nothing but the sound of the bathroom door closing. I peeked through the door. *Now!*

I grabbed my things and ran out the door, out of the floor, out of the elevator and out of the building. My only advantage was that I had always traveled light. Still, my backpack never felt so heavy and my grip on my carry-on was making my hand sore—I could not ease up on it.

I was running out the building's door when I saw Roland

opening the door of the Citroën and Miss Mary stepping out. He did not see me. I entered a coffee shop next to their building and watched them from behind the glass window as they crossed the old cobblestone alley. Roland held Miss Mary's arm gently, and walked her in to their building. At the building's tall, intricate iron doors, he stopped and looked behind him—nodding his head as if he knew he was being watched. Mary, perfectly coiffed, looked happy and elegant. They were happy together.

It took a while for me to take a breath again. My heart was racing and I felt like I was missing something. No, I wasn't missing anything. It was just emptiness, and I didn't know why.

As soon as they disappeared through the iron doors I ran out of the café and entered the first taxi that stopped for me.

"Chiado please," and I let the seat hug me as I ducked inside the car. I wanted to hide from the world, but the taxi driver was taking me through the narrow cobblestone streets that gave Lisbon its exhilarating character. I could not help but glance through the window. I felt very nostalgic to be there again. I loved Lisbon. I loved its people, and its secrets. Lisbon had been kind to me when I came back to it, searching for the evidence Douglas believed existed. And João, who had doubted that it could be true, played a big part in my discovery. It was all worth it and I can't wait to see his face when I show it to him.

Now, safe inside the taxi, it was as if the stay with Roland and Mary had never happened. I was back on track, and my destiny still awaited me, secretly tucked inside my bag.

Chapter 15

Hiding From Hate

THE NIGHT I PULLED THE TRIGGER on grandma's old rifle will haunt me forever. It is my nightmare. As I closed my eyes and pulled the trigger, I managed to put a bullet through his heart. Now, the only difference between us is that I'm still alive, and he is not. I had finally learned about hate.

I want one day to wake up and realize that it was only a dream, a very cruel dream. But instead, I recall the morning I woke up in the witches' living room with a vague remembrance of what I had done the night before.

It was from there, inside their room, that they had peeked at me over the years that I had passed outside their window. Now, lying on their sofa, I could see the cobblestone path where I walked everyday, and just like the witches did, I saw the girl who had grown into a woman.

It was right there, under their wings that I decided to move away. My little old town had become too small for me. I wanted to hide. Run away and forget. I did not know then, that I couldn't simply forget.

So, less than a month later, I packed the few things I owned, kissed my witches goodbye and closed the door of the pastel yellow house behind me. There, I left the beach where

Lucien held my hand. I left the saints singing over the church's bell where I walked by many times. I left the fishermen sitting on their canoes and I left the witches with their grayish eyes. With me, I took only sorrow, sorrow and dreams. For now it was all dreams. And so I was gone.

Chapter 16

Trapped By His Love

FLORIANÓPOLIS WAS A BEAUTIFUL PLACE to be—an island in the South, close to the mainland Brazil, where I was still lost hoping to redeem my sin someday.

There, I got a job working in a small restaurant where we served "the best fried fish on the island," as my boss used to say.

Most of my days were the same. Every morning, I took the same bus to town, with the same driver and the same people inside it. The people, they looked at me with questioning eyes. They wanted to know why I was there; they wanted to know what I was hiding from. I tried my best to ignore them, but my skin could feel their curious eyes staring at me, and I just sat there, quietly on my seat.

On the weekends I was on my own. There were no curious eyes and there was nothing to hide from. There, on the small beach town of Canasvieiras, walking on the white sand beach, I mourned my mother and the life I left behind, and slowly I came out a survivor.

In the summer days, the beach was crowded with exotic, lively people who wanted to get away from the big city and enjoy the warm sand beach, but in the winter, the white fine sand was left to the wind. The place became like a ghost town. If it weren't for the few local families who lived there year round and a couple of strays like me, the place would be deserted.

It was there, walking on its fine sand, when I was running away from my destiny that I saw him again, just as God had pre-ordained.

I had been there, living at the beach, when one afternoon I saw a fishing canoe dragging a net to the sand. As the canoe approached the shore, and the fishermen spoke rapidly among themselves, people started to crowd on the beach, chasing the net to help bring it in. I sat there on the sand contemplating the precision with which they were handling the net. I had never seen so many fish in my life and as the fishermen freed the catch, they made a huge pile of fish on the sand. I could hardly believe that the little canoe had dragged it all in.

The next day I sat on the white sand looking for the canoe again and I was thrilled when I saw it coming from the horizon. As the canoe approached the shore and the people got busy dragging the net in, I decided to help. I walked to the shore uncertain of what to expect, but the smile on people's faces told me that I was welcome. They started to show me what to do and soon I was freeing the fish from the net. It was a hard job but absolutely rewarding, especially when I realized that the pile of smaller fishes was placed back into the water.

It was just before nightfall and I was walking back home carrying the fish I had earned when he approached me.

"Do you know how to clean it?" he asked, looking at the fish I was holding by its tail. I did not believe my eyes.

Standing next to me, the sailor who I idolized and who had once called me "Sunshine" was smiling.

"Yes," I said, feeling nauseated, and sure that I was going to throw up.

He did not believe I could clean the fish and so he kept walking along my side. He asked if I took out the guts, or if I scaled it first. I stopped and looked at him again. Still feeling sick to my stomach, I told him that I chopped the head off first, which made him laugh.

I kept walking towards home and he kept following me as he mumbled about the different ways to clean the damn thing. My heart was beating fast and I did not know what to say, so I kept walking. He asked me how I was doing and if I was enjoying my stay, which in response, I just nodded and gave him a nervous smile.

He knew about me, just like everyone else did—the place knew I had arrived.

As I walked down the beach with him by my side I realized that he did not remember me from his visits to the Pacific Bakery.

Of course not! I had grown up and had turned into a woman. No, he did not remember the girl who he had called "Sunshine."

He told me that his name was Douglas, which made me smile, because I finally realized he had a name. The name did suit him, I thought, remembering how fascinated I used to be by him.

Douglas was from Argentina, and he was in Florianópolis

because his boat was being repaired at the town's harbor.

He asked me about what brought me there, and why I was alone, but I ignored his questions and changed the subject. My heart then was starting to slow down and Douglas was becoming real.

Douglas confided to me that he had left his home and that he was sailing alone. He told me that he had a daughter back in Buenos Aires who was already married and had a family of her own. When I asked him about his wife he answered:

"She let me go."

He added that he was water and she was earth, and that the earth was always dry so they agreed to go on with their separate lives. He told me that he had been a history professor at the University of Buenos Aires, and that he had a sabbatical year to run up the coast of Brazil to do some sort of research, which I did not understand. He told me that his sabbatical year had turned into six, and that still he wasn't going home anytime soon.

"That's why I'm here," he said, "and I don't know how much longer I'll stay. It all depends on the people at the harbor." And he pondered. "They work very slowly," he said not looking too concerned.

He smiled showing his big square smile, which I had not forgotten, and he told me that he was not too worried since he was enjoying his stay at the beach. He said that he had tried to help the men at the harbor, but every time he went down to check on the progress, the men just told him, "No worries, it will be done next week."

"This has been going on for a couple of weeks now, but the men still haven't touched my boat," he said with a look on his face which told me that there was no hope for his sailboat to be ready anytime soon.

He told me all this while helping me clean the fish in my small kitchen—since he wanted to make sure I knew what I was doing with the thing.

"From now on," he said, "you will always come home with a fresh catch in hand," and he ran the knife on the fish's stomach making it bleed. "You won't bring the net only once. Now, you will be caught bringing it every evening and they will always thank you with a fish."

That night, after Douglas left, I lay in bed for hours without being able to sleep. I remembered my days working at the bakery. I remembered the days that he walked in and the world seemed to stop. I remembered the day he left and I remembered why I was alone. I finally fell asleep but soon woke up to the sounds of the bullets. It was my nightmare.

Chapter 17

Too Much Fish

THE NEXT DAY it was just like Douglas said it would be. I could not help but walk to the shore and help the fishermen and their families bring in the net. Like I said, it was hard work, but I liked it. All that fish in the net . . . all the people I met, it all made Canasvieiras a very pleasant place to be. But still, I did not forget what I had done, even though I was starting to feel happy again.

Every night, after the hard work of bringing in the heavy net, which after a few days left my hands bleeding, Douglas walked me home and made sure I was ok. Now, I had finally learned how to properly clean a fish, but still, I chopped the head off first, which Douglas didn't agree with.

"Too much fish is not good for you," he said, and so, some nights, he would bring Italian sausages and prepare us a very tasty pasta dish. While preparing the food Douglas would tell me amusing stories from his time teaching at the University in Buenos Aires and I would marvel at his knowledge, but when he mentioned his family he would have a very nostalgic look on his face, which told me somehow he missed them.

It wasn't expected, but soon, our nights became packed with history lessons, which I discovered to be very interesting.

On my bistro style table in the little kitchen in Canasvieiras, maps, books and note pads were scattered and Douglas started to entertain me with fabulous stories. And I, with stupefied eyes, I kept listening to him, without guessing that those were lessons he had actually prepared for me. He wanted me to learn, I had become his pupil, and I didn't know why.

Douglas was a lover; a lover of history, and just now, I realized that. There is simply no other way to describe him. His love for history made him leave his home and his family. He was lost in a far world—a world that had been forgotten—and this I realized within a few nights of listening to his lectures. Still, I let him seduce me into that world. He sounded brave. He sounded smart. But I felt that there was something that he was carrying on his shoulders, something weighing him down. Something he needed to let go, but I did not know what, not yet.

Cabral, Columbus, Cook, Magellan, all of a sudden my tiny world turned upside down. From the bottom of the Earth to the Alaskan seaways, Douglas taught me all about the world's discoveries. I was becoming familiar with the great explorers, their ways, and their findings, and at times, I found myself right there—on the new Terra, on the new land. Douglas needed to teach and he found in me the perfect pupil. Nothing escaped, and I looked forward to the evenings, to be with him—to listen to him. He taught me everything, but he failed to teach me what to do now that I was in possession of it.

Chapter 18

Losing It

 Back in Lisbon, 1991 ───

WHEN I ENTERED THE OLD LEATHER SHOP on the *Rua dos Correeiros*, my eyes caught a dusty picture tacked on the wall behind leather jackets, belts and shoes. It was a picture of Douglas and João. With arms over each other's shoulders, standing with huge grins on their faces, they stood in front of the Belém Tower, looking very grand themselves. It was such a wonderful scene, and Douglas started to make sense to me.

"Old fool," João said, when he saw me staring at the dusty picture.

How young were they? I could not help but wonder. Douglas wore the same style reading glasses and was dressed in old discolored bell-bottoms. His beautiful square smile, which made him so distinct, was stamped on his face. And now, looking at João, I see that he had not changed much. His graying hair and the wise look he carried in his eyes differentiated him from the young man, which he once was, to the man standing in front of me.

The picture was dusty and fading with time.

João picked up the picture from the wall and started to clean it with the handkerchief he took out of his pocket.

"I told him it was impossible," João said, looking at the picture in his hands. "But he was too stubborn," João said finishing cleaning the picture frame and hanging it back between the jackets.

João and Douglas had met in the city of Coimbra in the central region of Portugal. It had been more than thirty years ago. They had just entered law school and their friendship was an instant one. Soon, the young and wild men spent their nights tasting wine on the streets of town while revealing their life passions to each other. They were daring, young and fearless. They dropped out of university and started on their adventure backpacking around Europe. They only ceased travelling once they ran out of money. On their journey throughout the Old World, they explored famous museums and art galleries. They visited old kingdoms and they spent hours savoring European coffee, while conversing with different people.

Douglas was passionate about history and João about art. They were in law school because they felt obligated to fulfill their families' traditions, but they were feeling oppressed by not following their own dreams. Once they combined forces, nothing stopped them from following their ambitions. They became their own knights.

In Portugal, João took Douglas to the Castelo de São Jorge, to the Convento de Mafra and to the Palácio da Pena, which Douglas told me so much about. They drove south to Sagres, where supposedly a Portuguese Prince, named Henrique, started the first Portuguese navigation school. Douglas insisted on going there because he had heard about it. He was an avid sailor and he didn't want to go back to Argentina without visiting the historical site.

While in Portugal, Douglas embraced the Portuguese people, their traditions and history as if it were his own. And when he went back to Argentina he studied history, which had been his obsession.

His Portuguese friend João entered art school in Lisbon, but never finished it, preferring to open his own leather business.

Watching João hang the picture back in its place, I had to sit in an old rocking chair to catch my breath.

"I was waiting for you last night," he told me sounding worried.

"It is complicated João," I said, still gazing at the picture.

"You could have called."

"I am sorry," I said, feeling exhausted.

"Come here, give me a hug," and he reached for my tired and beat body.

We hugged for what seemed an eternity, and I cried. I cried and could not stop sobbing. João just hugged me until I finally had no more tears. He too had tears in his eyes. We were mourning Douglas together.

He closed the atelier door and hung the sign that said "Be Back Soon" on it. João led me through a narrow hallway to the back of his shop. At the end of it, a door opened to a veranda where a few tables and chairs sat under canvas umbrellas. He called it his little haven in the city. There, he shared the veranda with the café next door.

The bougainvilleas were blooming, and the afternoon sun was just starting to hide behind the building next door. João left me there—where I was mesmerized with the hidden place, and half lost in my thoughts. He walked in to the café next door and came back with two espressos. I had stopped crying, but still, I could not say a thing.

"I told the fool it couldn't be done," João said, placing the espressos on the table in front of me.

"I told him it was too dangerous to risk everything, but he wanted it anyway, didn't he?" João said, swallowing his espresso.

"Wait, João," I said, and I walked back into the atelier and got my burgundy carry-on. I came back to the veranda and placed it on the table. I opened it very carefully and my heart stopped.

"Son of a bitch," I managed to yell. *How could I have been so stupid?*

Chapter 19

Drifting Away

IT WAS FEBRUARY OF 1988, when the Royal Cruise Line announced on Brazil's television that they were hiring. I thought it was an opportunity I could not miss. I was twenty years old, I was hiding away from my guilt, and trying to forget what I had done, but still, it was not far enough . . . and Douglas? I could not fathom a life without him. I knew that he too would leave me soon. It was that or nothing, and so I decided to apply for the job.

"No, it is a surprise," I told the witches on the phone, when I called them to say that I was going to be leaving to Rio de Janeiro for a job interview. I was so excited that my application had been selected that I had to share it with someone.

The interview was going to be at the cruise line's offices in Rio. I was thrilled but at the same time worried, because I had never been to Rio before.

The witches, they were my connection to my past; they were part of the good things I left behind. They knew my misfortune, and somehow, I felt empowered knowing that they approved of what I had done.

They were happy to hear from me, but concerned about what I was up to. I told them not to worry and that if everything worked out, I would go visit them soon. It was all that I said, but Carmen, the youngest of them all, the one who had caused the curse to haunt them, said that she would come see me before I left for the interview.

I hung up the phone and thought that it was funny that Carmen was coming to visit, but excited because I missed her so much. She was the one who touched my burning face as I stepped out of the stuffy closet after killing the monster that killed my Mother. She was the one to take me in.

The days prior to my witch's arrival were consumed with expectations about working on the cruise. I imagined all the wonderful places I would go and things I would see, and of course, I did not think about the work. No, not at all! In my mind, it was going to be a fantastic vacation, where I would finally be able to see the world, but first—I had to be hired.

My anxiety grew larger the night before Carmen arrived. I didn't sleep much that night, since Douglas and I spent hours talking and looking at history books, which he had brought to show me.

I enjoyed Douglas's company. He was funny, sarcastic, and at times scary, but my heart told me that he was not going to hurt me. No matter what, he was there to actually look after me, and before he left for his place that night I told him that my friend Carmen was arriving in the morning.

"Finally I will meet someone close to the most amazing young lady I have ever met," he said, making me blush. He kissed me good night and walked into the dark where I could see his tall silhouette vanishing away. I wondered. I wondered about the day when his sail would blow again, and my heart would sink. *I have to get the job.*

I needed Douglas. I barely knew him but he made me feel safe. Our relationship was something out of this world. If one had seen it, one would not understand. He was the fearless wanderer who happened to become my protector, and I? I became the dreamer wonderer, who had no idea of what he was doing to me, and what was to come.

I fell asleep in the early morning, but soon was awakened by the sunrays sneaking through my storm window. I got up, ate something fast, and took the bus to go meet the witch in town. I was thrilled to see her. She approved of what I had done, and she never questioned me, just like I never questioned her about the curse of being called a witch. She knew that I would probably be dead if I had not pulled the trigger on grandma's rifle.

On the bus ride to my apartment, she told me about how they missed us, and how the place was not the same anymore without me walking in front of their home with my curious eyes. I felt tears fighting to escape from my eyes, but I kept myself strong, not adding to our sorrow.

I told her about the job I was applying for, and I told her about Douglas. I told her all about what I was learning with him, and she smiled. It was as if I didn't need to tell her anything.

She knew that I was on my way out, and that I wanted a

one-way ticket. She knew I wanted to see beyond the horizon, beyond the dirt road where grandma's fort sat, and beyond the cold cobblestone where their house sat facing the road.

As Douglas entered the door of my little beach house the night Carmen arrived, he was truly happy to meet her. But Carmen, she looked like she didn't know what to think of him.

"He is just a friend," I told her ignoring the look in her face as soon as he left us alone in the kitchen. But evidently she already knew the truth. He was more than a friend. He was my redeemer.

The tension was broken when Douglas said to her, "Marina will do big things with her life."

Carmen's face lightened up. I was, after all, her favorite girl.

"Yes, she will!" she affirmed with a smile from ear to ear, easily accepting whatever relationship Douglas and I were having. "She is brave like a man," she told him.

I can't believe she just said that. Those were Mom's words! Why do they think that for one to do big things in life, one must be a man? my mind asked me, raging.

Instead of showing her my disappointment about the insulting comment, I tried to ignore it since we were having a very pleasant night and I didn't want to spoil it.

Until that moment Douglas didn't know that I was leaving for Rio de Janeiro for the job interview. I did not want to tell him. Not yet. But of course the witch managed to spill it out.

"Yes, she will do great things," she said. "Even more now that she is going to work on a ship," she said proud.

Instead of continuing on his way out, Douglas turned

and walked back to the chair where he had been comfortably sitting most of the night and sat down again.

I noticed his body tensing. He did not ask a question, but I knew that his mind was troubling him. It had been only a few months since we had met but I knew that something was disturbing his mind. He continued talking to Carmen as if he had not heard what she had said, and did not look at me the rest of the night, ignoring my presence.

I regretted not mentioning the job, but it was too late because Douglas was acting very strange.

Shit, Carmen! I thought. *Why did you have to say it*? I asked in vain.

After what seemed an eternity of Carmen and Douglas throwing words away, he got up from the chair said good night and walked to the door. I followed him just like I had done night after night since we had started on our journey. He turned back to me, kissed my forehead, and holding my face between his hands, he told me that we would talk later. My eyes were fixed to his, and I knew that he had much to say or to ask but I was glad he didn't do so. Not yet.

The next morning, my witch went back to her life and I was alone again. I realized then, that that was it. I was free to follow my destiny.

That evening as the sun was sinking, I sat on the white sand and I cried. Through my blurry eyes I saw the canoe coming from the horizon but instead of walking to the shore and helping the fishermen, I walked back home. That was the last time I saw the canoe coming to shore.

Chapter 20

And So I Learned That He Was Mad

THE NIGHT I FOUND OUT that Douglas was mad was just like every other night. We just did our thing—he cooked dinner, and I cleaned the kitchen while he sat outside on the veranda looking into the space, waiting to start with our lesson. It was the night before I left for the interview with the cruise line.

That night, as Douglas showed me the route of a Portuguese sailor who went searching the world hunting for riches, I felt that Douglas was irritated. Something was bothering him. I too was apprehensive since he had not mentioned the fact that I was leaving. I wanted his approval before going to the interview; I wanted him to tell me that it was all right, tell me to go for it. But instead, I just sat there listening to him, the same way I had done every night.

His lessons were becoming my passion, and time seemed to fly when we were together. Douglas was taking me on amazing adventures and I felt as if the world was in the palm of my hand. It seemed so small, so close, but so far fetched.

Douglas was a captivating storyteller, and I had started to have wild daydreams about the stories he told me. He told me stories of explorations, conquests and despairs. Stories of what men had encountered on their search for the unknown.

But where am I going with all this? I asked myself many times, just to find no answer to it.

That night, as Douglas' fingers travelled the old map, which was lying on my table, they stopped at the very tip of South America. He looked into my eyes with begging hope. It was a look I had not seen on his face before, and I wondered about the next story he was going to tell me.

He took off his thick glasses, which were hanging on his nose, and rubbed his eyes. He tried to stretch his large body but the bench attached to the kitchen table did not give him enough space and so he got up and walked outside, again . . . looking into the nothing. Douglas put his glasses back on his nose and walked back in to the kitchen where I was still sitting on the bench and leaning on the table, contemplating the old map. Douglas sat on the bench next to me, making me nervous—he had never done that before. His large body was touching mine, making me tense. It was a strange feeling to have him that close to me, since he had sat across the table all the nights we had spent together in my little kitchen.

Douglas leaned his elbow on the table, rested his face on his hand and stared at me. It seemed that he was analyzing my features, or maybe trying to read my mind. It was the first time we had been that close and I could smell the exotic fragrance emanating from his body. *Maybe it had not been a good thing after all, to let this stranger into my life and into my house.*

"What is it?" I asked trying to distract him from whatever thoughts he was contemplating.

He closed his eyes and turned his head to the map on the table. Slowly he opened his eyes again, and though the rugged map was lying in front of him I could tell that he was not seeing it. His eyes were focused much further than inside my little kitchen at the apartment on the beach of Canasvieiras. Whatever he was looking at was far beyond what I could imagine.

My anticipation was growing wild, and I didn't know what to make of the situation. Until then, Douglas had been the fort I found at sea, but now, I wasn't sure anymore.

"Can you keep secrets?" he asked me.

His eyes then had the same grayish look I had seen in the witches' eyes and they were glued to mine. All of a sudden I felt as if cold ice was running its way through my body, where it started to melt and I started to sweat.

"Sure," I said, not certain.

He touched my arm with his strong hand and wrapped his long lean fingers around it. He held it tight for a second, then eased up on it as his eyes dropped again to the old map.

"Maybe not," I said freeing my arm from his hand.

My heart was beating fast—making it difficult to catch my breath. My mind was confused.

Maybe he is not a bad guy. Maybe he is just a little crazy; I tried to convince myself. Still, my heart was racing, and the sweat, which would become familiar to me, was taking over.

As he looked at the old faded map again I felt his body

relaxing a bit. His fingers touched the map and caressed it, following to the bottom of South America—turning into the big Pacific Ocean. Suddenly he stopped and looked at me again.

"His name was Magellan. Ferdinand Magellan," Douglas said. "He was the Portuguese man I told you about," and he took a deep breath. "The one who offered to work for the Spanish crown after his own king denied him a life at sea."

"Yes, I remember," I agreed, confused.

Douglas looked at me again and now the look in his eyes was different from all the looks he had shown me before. Douglas was alive.

"It is believed that Magellan was killed in the Philippines, which are some islands in the Pacific. Here," he said, placing his finger over the mass of land on the old map that had sacrificed so much to us.

He showed me the location of the islands and continued with my lesson, but now speaking faster and clearer.

"It is also believed that Magellan died without leaving any records of his final journey," Douglas told me. "Some historians suggest that Magellan never wrote in a log while on his search for a way to the Orient through the West." Douglas paused and looked enraged. "It is all crap," Douglas said and continued, "The only known accounts of his voyage are through the journal of a young Italian sailor who survived the expedition and made it back to Spain. In his journal, the young lad describes Magellan as being his lord—'The one who could see beyond obstacles,'" Douglas told me.

"Magellan was a brave and fierce man and he lived at a time when the rush for riches and power was ruling the world. It was a time when religious beliefs were being forced onto men, and a time, when one was judged by his fortune and status. Magellan believed that there was a passage leading to the spices through the South of America. Spices, at that time, were worth more than gold, and if Magellan found a way to get there, he would find richness and glory, enter the Spanish high society, and become his own lord. But what I believe is that he wanted to prove to his old Portuguese king that he was still worthy of a life at sea."

I did not have a clue where his mind was going and why he was dragging me with it. *Yes, it is just another story, of another one of his heroes,* I told myself. *But this time he is much more obsessed than usual.*

"What history suggests is not true, you know?" he said, looking at me with hope in his eyes, begging me to believe in his madness. "Magellan died, but he did leave records of his last voyage."

No. I did not know. How could I?

All I knew until I met Douglas was my little world in which I lived.

The bakery.

My white sand beach.

A dark closet.

Three bullets.

How does he expect me to know all this?

He is crazy! I told myself, and I knew that it wasn't the

best time to tell him that I was leaving the next day to Rio de Janeiro for my job interview, but I did it anyway.

Ah! How I regret doing it at that time.

Douglas punched the table where the old map was resting and yelled at me in a rage, "Why are you telling me this only now?" and he got up from the table and started to walk back and forth in the little kitchen.

"I . . . I thought I would let you know . . . but . . . I . . . I didn't think it was a big deal," I said trying to contain the tears fighting to get out of my eyes.

"How long have you known this?" his voice was raised again.

"For a couple of weeks, but I don't even know if I am getting the job," I said. "Besides, you will be leaving as soon as your boat is ready, and I . . . I don't want to be here after you leave," I confessed, letting the tears fall on my face down to my lips.

That was it—I didn't want to be there after Douglas was gone. I wanted to run away. Run away and fast! I realized that as soon as he was able to lift his sail, I was going to sink like an anchor, deep into soft sand, and I knew that I would not have the strength to surface again—not after he left.

Douglas walked outside to the veranda and continued to pace back and forth. When I noticed he looking at me I turned my face away. I was afraid to reveal my weakness.

I heard him coming back into the kitchen and he stood close to me. His hand touched my shoulder and I looked at him. He touched my face and leaned his large body to embrace me. He dried my tears and I let my body fall into his arms.

"I am a selfish bastard!" He said, touching my hair and keeping me in his arms.

I felt defeated.

It had been the first time I had broken down since my mother died.

Douglas waited for me to stop sobbing and gently pushed me away from him, touching my face and drying my last tears.

"How could I do this to you?" he said, and gently hugged me again.

We walked onto the veranda and I sat next to him where the sky above us opened the door for my confession. "Douglas," I said, fighting the knot in my throat which was trying to shut me up. "Do you know why I am here? Do you know why I am alone?" and I told him everything.

I had to tell him. I had to tell someone. I needed someone to tell me that it was all right. I needed his approval. I needed him to understand me and help me to understand myself. I told him that I did not just want to be. I wanted to live. I told him about my being, my needs, and my fears. Paralyzed, sitting across from me, Douglas listened to my confession.

As I recalled the stuffy closet and the sound of the bullets, I felt light. I told him that my mind was disturbed because I didn't regret what I had done. I told him that if I had not killed the man I would not be there with him that day. I told him that the only remorse I felt was not having a mother anymore, and for that, I hated the man even more. I told him that I did not feel guilty for killing, and that I would do it again and again.

I was supposed to feel guilty. After all, being a good Catholic girl, that's what I was raised to believe. I told him that I was finally free, and that he had contributed to it. I told him that if I had met him through different circumstances I would probably not feel as confused, but I also told him that I believed that it was my destiny. I understood that I had my life to live, and that what I left behind was just a chapter of my big life. I told him that I didn't understand why I was so eager to keep moving, and I told him that since his lessons, I had become obsessed with discovering the world, which he was revealing to me. I was eager to see what was there to be seen. I did not even know how big my world was. Besides the old map lying on my kitchen table, I had not a clue of how far one could go. I told him that I wanted to see it all, and he understood me. He said it was my fate, it was my fortune, and he said I was doing the right thing.

He swore at all that I had lived through. He said he wished I were his daughter. He also said that if I were his, he would never have left me.

"I had no right to treat you the way I did," he said taking his glasses off his nose and rubbing his tired eyes. "I am sorry," he said, and got up and went to the kitchen to start water for our tea.

After telling him the truth about why I was alone in the world, I felt as if a massive weight had left my shoulders. I even smiled and told him all about the job for which I was applying.

"So, I guess you are finally going to see the world," he said with a slight smile.

"Well . . . yes," I answered. "But first I have to be hired. Guess where the cruise is going?" I asked him trying to sound flirty.

He raised his eyebrows waiting for me to tell him.

"Portugal." I told him, as if I had already been hired. "The land of your Magellan!"

My words were like a punch in the air. The moment froze in time. Now I recall it all in slow motion as I remember the way Douglas received the news. Somehow I had only seen half of the man Douglas was, for at that moment his other half came alive, and I was there to see it being reborn.

"I knew it. I knew it all the time," he said looking at me with a big grin on his face, which perplexed me.

"The day I saw you at the bakery, I knew I wasn't alone. But then, you were still too young. Too fragile."

Wait a minute. So he did recognize me?

"I wanted then to tell you about the world that was out there. I knew you were craving it. But I was too ashamed of myself, and of the irony, which had being playing with me. But I knew. I knew you were the one." Douglas said.

He remembers me.

And knowing what he was doing to me he said, "You are going to do big things." and he walked to my kitchen sink and poured hot water over our tea bags.

That night, we sat around the table, among the books and maps on its surface, and we did not sleep. Douglas spent all night guiding me through the routes opened by seafarers hundreds of years before my time. He did not miss a thing. Douglas talked fast and I took notes. His eyes were mischievous, alive. It reminded me of my own eyes, looking at the chicken, which was going to be killed by Grandma, back in her dirt yard, where my fort faced the sunset—my mind troubled while she ran for the kill. *Please don't let the chicken suffer.*

"This is a big fish Marina. I promise you, you won't regret doing me this favor," Douglas said, encouraging me.

Chapter 21

Out of the River

AFTER DOUGLAS GRADUATED from college in Buenos Aires, he went back to Portugal to pursue a Master's degree in history. There he was welcomed by his friend João, who had become his accomplice in life.

Douglas had decided on a thesis based on the Portuguese navigators. He managed to combine his love for the sea and his love for history into one big experience.

He said that while he was in Portugal studying for his Masters, he spent hours at the Museu da Marinha by the River Tejo in Lisbon, collecting data for his thesis. He also told me that he spent hours on the docks by the river, looking for boat rides around the bay. He told me that he loved to sink himself into the books and logs of the explorers, and afterwards go for long walks by the river, where he found warmth among the boats resting on its waters.

Douglas told me that in one of those walks, an ordinary scene caught his attention. He saw a young kid jumping off a sailboat into the cool waters of the River Tejo. What looked common around the docks startled Douglas as he noticed how comfortable the boy was in the water.

"Get back here right now, or I will never let you work with your grandpa again," a beautiful lady yelled to the young boy. It looked as if the boy was seriously going to cause her to have a heart attack.

Douglas told me that the kid, who had looked very comfortable in the cool water, crawled back into the boat. The lady, who had been hyperventilating a moment before, wrapped the young man in a towel and covered the youth's face with kisses.

Douglas said that as he approached the boat where the boy was now, safe and dry, an older man yelled to the youngster from the dock's parking lot. The man, juggling boxes and bags of supplies, wanted the boy to come and help him.

Douglas said that as he saw the man struggling with the boxes and bags, he crossed the lot and lent the old man a hand.

"With a growing kid on board, we have to make sure there is enough food," the man joked, throwing his chin in the direction of the sailboat with the lady and the child on it.

"I can see that he has a lot of energy," Douglas told the man. "He can swim well too," Douglas said, and he walked with the man to the sailboat placing the boxes he had helped carry on the deck.

"Oh yes, little Land has been in these waters since he was a baby." the old man said. "He better know how to swim," he assured with a proud look on his face.

"Do you know how many times I have had to go looking for him just to find that he had swam all the way to the ship wreck?" the man asked Douglas while juggling the grocery bags onto the deck. "Yes", the man said. "My boy knows how to swim," the man continued, sounding confident of the young protégé's skills.

The man, Douglas thought, was probably in his fifties, and the boy next to him could not be more than thirteen. Douglas dropped the last box on the deck and was about to say goodbye when the lady, who had stopped covering the boy's face with kisses, invited him for a drink.

He accepted the invitation and made his way through the boxes lying around the deck, while the old man was busy carrying a few more bags inside.

Douglas sat down across from where the boy was busy, opening some clams, and marveled at the precision with which the young lad handled the shells. Douglas told them that he had been in Lisbon for a couple of months and that he had been lucky finding rides around the bay.

"Too bad we are not sailing the bay," yelled the old man from below, where he was busy organizing the supplies. "We are leaving for a couple of days and another set of hands would be nice. Wouldn't it, Land?" the man asked the young boy.

The kid stopped opening the shells and took a long doubting look at Douglas, and then continued to do his job. He offered Douglas a big piece of meat, which he had scooped from a shell, and Douglas swallowed the raw thing in one gulp. Douglas believed that that convinced the kid.

"Yes, grandpa. I guess it would be ok," and he winked at Douglas and continued to dig the meat out of the shells.

The lady's name was Mary. She told Douglas that it was their tradition to sail on the week of the anniversary of the Portuguese discoveries. She told him that they were on their way to Sagres.

"Have you been there?" she asked Douglas, and without giving him time to answer, she continued; "It is a must. It's grandpa's favorite place, and our Land likes it there too. Right Land?"

Douglas told her that he had not been in Sagres since his attempt at law school, six years before.

He told Miss Mary that he was in Portugal studying for his master's degree and that he was researching the Portuguese Navigators. He also said that he would not be leaving Portugal before going back to Sagres to visit the site of the Navigation School, founded by Prince Henrique.

"Why don't you come with us?" said the boy who was growing out of his voice and who was looking at his grandpa for consent.

"Yes, why not?" said Mary, from under her sailing hat. "There is always room for one more sea lover in our *Estrela do Mar.*"

Douglas recalled that Mr. Manuel looked at him and did not hesitate to say, "Yes, come on. It will be fun."

Douglas was thrilled and accepted the invitation. After all, he had nothing to do in the next few days since the entire country would be shut down for the celebrations. The museum where he conducted most of his research would be closed, and his friend João, had gone to Óbidos, to be with family.

"Let's go," said João, when he was leaving Lisbon on his way to the family home in Óbidos, but Douglas was determined to stay in Lisbon and told his friend that he would be fine spending the holiday alone, and now, that he had been invited to join in on the *Estrela do Mar*, on the trip to Sagres, Douglas was sure that he had made the right decision.

Douglas told Mr. Manuel that he needed some time to go grab a few things since he wasn't prepared for the trip. The man agreed to wait for him and Douglas rushed out from the dock, just to come back shortly after, with a few changes of clothes.

On the *Estrela do Mar*, as they sailed past the shipwreck on the River Tejo, the grandpa said that it was a shame that the old vessel had perished. Now, popping out of the water, the ship was showing vestiges of rusting metal.

As the city fell behind them, Douglas could see the Castelo de São Jorge sitting on the hill behind old Lisbon.

Towards the left of the city was the Bairro Alto where Douglas sat many nights with his friend João, contemplating the beauty of the old cobblestoned streets and its people. Bairro Alto was one of Douglas' favorite places. It was there that literary types, college students, yuppies, artists and passionate people with all sorts of desires spent most of their time. There, one could see the classic Portuguese men, sitting on their chairs by the door of their homes, staring at their own neighborhood without making a sound.

There, the bohemians talked to the statue of Fernando Pessoa, the Portuguese poet who sang the country's history. There, the beautiful Portuguese women, with their carefree style, called attention without even noticing the impact they made on the population. There, the young and handsome men laughed without shame while puffing on their cigarettes, which completed their charming style. Youngsters dressed in the latest fashion, walked tall with entitlement to their world. How could it be? So much contrast, in so much harmony? They all contributed to the glamour of the place, making it alluring. It was a place unknown to the outside world, but a world of its own.

Douglas was happy to have met João. And now he was happy to meet the Medeiros. On their sailboat with the cool breeze helping the drifting vessel, Douglas felt invincible. He described it as an emotion incomparable to any other. He was sailing south to where the first Portuguese seamen oppressed by land deprivation, started Magellan's dream—the dream of a man who thought he could conquer the world.

Little did Douglas know then—if he could just fathom what awaited him he may have never boarded that ship, for what he was seduced to, ruled the rest of his life. When Douglas came back from his trip to the South with Miss Mary, Mr. Manuel and little Land, he came back a changed man, and, as soon as he landed, he went to João's atelier.

As Douglas entered the leather shop, he noticed that João had hung the picture of them, standing in front of the Torre de Belém in Lisbon, on the wall of his shop. He smiled as he saw it and continued to the back of the shop. João hung the sign that said "Be Back Soon" on the front door at the Rua dos Correeiros and followed Douglas to the veranda next to the café, where they ordered two coffees and two Absyntos. There, where they called it their haven in the city, they talked for hours. It took Douglas the rest of the afternoon to convince João that he was into something.

"*Shoots* man," said João intrigued by what he had learned from Douglas. "If you can prove it man, you will change history," João told Douglas, who could not stay sitting in his chair from excitement.

As he explained what he had learned from little Land's grandpa on the trip to the South, his hands talked as much as his lips. Every few minutes he wiped his forehead, even though the weather was cool in October. Douglas' enthusiasm was contagious and João said to Douglas that he was going to take the next few days to help him in the hunt for any evidence. After all, he came to believe, just like Douglas, that Magellan didn't die without leaving any records of his voyages.

But why? They asked. Why are there secrets?

Who would do such a thing and why?

Chapter 22

The Lost Evidence

AFTER OPENING MY BURGUNDY CARRY-ON in the back of João's shop and coming to the cruel realization that Roland had stolen it from me, I ran out of the door leaving João behind. I had been cheated. I couldn't believe that I had let him do that to me.

I walked on the streets trying to make sense of what had happened, but it all felt out of focus. I wanted to know why Roland had stolen it from me, and I wanted what was mine back. I knew that the answer might be found sometime six years ago—the night before I left for my interview with the cruise line, when Douglas told me about Magellan's secret. Douglas believed it existed.

"But Douglas . . . " I remember arguing with him. "How do you know it exists?"

"I just know, ok," he would say.

"But Douglas . . . how do you know you are right? It is my life that will be at risk," I said, not believing what he had just asked me. "Just because you believe it, there is no justification for what you are asking me," I told him feeling confused.

Douglas looked deep again into my eyes. It was the same

look he used to give me when he wanted to tell me something grand.

I turned my back to him because I did not want to hear what he was going to say, and that's when he blurted it out.

"If you really want to know, I will tell you."

I turned back facing him and pleaded with my eyes for him not to tell me what I didn't want to know—I was afraid.

But he did. He did it anyway. He told me what he wanted me to hear. He needed to share his madness.

Did he know what he was doing to me? Did he realize that I was only a girl trying to move on with my mediocre life? No, he didn't. Douglas had bigger plans for my life. He had bigger plans for me.

Douglas continued telling me what he wanted me to know. What he believed.

"What history suggests is not true. It is not true because there is a letter that Magellan sent to his Portuguese friend Serrão. He wrote the letter while on his last voyage. In that letter, he told his friend that he was probably making a mistake staying in South America for the winter. However, he was forced to stay since he had waited too long, undecided whether or not to continue on his search, and the bad weather did not permit him to sail any further. In the letter, he told his friend the reason he was staying through the winter in such a precarious and dangerous place was worth much more than the spices. He told Serrão that on the back of the letter was a map of a land, which he believed he would find. There is also another letter that Magellan wrote to his beloved wife, who was waiting for his return back to Spain. One will never know which letter was written first because the letter to his friend was not dated. The letters have disappeared from the Portuguese archives, and the answer to the map, which Magellan drew for his friend, is in the letter he wrote to his wife. In the letter, he told her about a land below the ice; a land Magellan believed existed further south. He told her that he had met the people who once resided there. It was there, on the edge of South America, where Magellan was searching for the passage that could possibly lead him to the spices that he landed and exchanged with the people. It was a custom to offer goods upon their arrival at new places, and in exchange, the people offered presents to the visitors. They welcomed Magellan, and because they had their feet wrapped in large bundles of leather to protect them from the cold weather, Magellan called them *Patagóns*, which explains why today they are called Patagonians. Magellan mingled among the people and before he continued on his search for the passage, which he believed existed; the *Patagóns* gave Magellan a gold coin, which he sent to his wife with the letter he wrote her. On that gold coin a figure of a woman is depicted. When Magellan asked the *Patagóns* where the coin had come from, they pointed to the South. Magellan was puzzled since all he could see was a raging sea and bergs of ice floating on it. However, Magellan understood that the reason why these people were persevering in the cold land was because they believed that one day the sun would melt the unforgiving ice and their forbidden kingdom would rise again. Magellan told his wife that he believed that they were talking about the long lost continent. He believed it was the same land he heard stories about when he was only a teenager, serving as a pageboy for the Portuguese Queen Leonor. He told his wife, that the ice covering it, played games with his eyes, and he said that he would not leave until he was able to see it.

In his letter he said:

My love,

You, who have seen the best and the worst of me, please believe in my words, for I know it is not the imagination of an old dreamer. You, who have entrusted the rest of your life to be with me, please be the one to understand my agony, for without your understanding the sea will remain my home. Tell me please that you trust me; this will be enough for me to continue on my hunt. For man must know the truth, where the lost land sits at the end of the South, where ice covers its crevices, debilitating it from rising again; the empire which once was, and that for now I believe I may find. You my love, you and my Brother Serrão are the only ones to know it.

Forever yours,

Fernão.

"This same man did not die leaving the world empty of his wisdom. The letter he wrote to his wife, together with the coin he sent her, the Jesuits in Rio de Janeiro have possession of it, and now, I need to find the letter he sent to his friend Serrão."

I cursed him. I cursed Douglas for trusting me with his madness.

"How do you know this is real and that this all really happened?" I asked furiously.

"I know it because I tried to steal it once," Douglas told me without remorse.

"The letter never arrived to his beloved wife and she died without knowing how much he trusted and loved her. There must also be a diary somewhere. A diary with Magellan's logs, which I believe, tells the exact location where the lost land sits. The only problem is . . . " he paused, "I don't know where it is."

God damm it!

"It must be somewhere," he continued in his rage, "and we must find it."

What does he means by "we?"

I remember that Douglas had told me that he believed that Magellan's log was lost after Magellan's death in the Philippines, and that the Portuguese, who were the enemies of Spain at the time, captured one of the ships left from the expedition—the ship that Magellan had commanded.

"On the reports of the few men who survived the expedition, it is said that they burned Magellan's belongings after their captain died. Again, I don't buy it. The men were probably afraid to tell the Spanish king that they had lost Magellan's log—together with the ship. No, it must be somewhere. Someone must have it."

A chill ran through my body. Something was terribly wrong.

He was not only crazy but he was also a thief. I didn't have time to finish processing my thoughts when I heard him say, "Now it is your turn to try to steal it," and he looked and sounded as if he had just given me the greatest news of my life.

"The Jesuits have a monastery in Rio de Janeiro where they keep many secrets hidden within their walls. There is a room called *Padre* José de Anchieta. You must get there," he said, "pay a visit to the Jesuits, get the letter Magellan wrote to his wife, and then leave. You will board that cruise and nobody will ever know what you did," Douglas told me, as if it were as simple as that. "I have tried, but the priests are too smart by now, they know I am after something. They won't open up to me," he said. "But you? they will let you in. You will think of something smart. You find the letter and bring it to me."

Did Douglas just ask me to steal for him?

Of course he did.

Chapter 23

Meeting My Assassin, 1991

I WENT BACK TO MARY'S APARTMENT and knocked on the door—the same door she had opened the night before, when I arrived with Roland.

"Oh honey, there you are," Mary said when she opened the door. "I thought you were not coming back."

"I told you she would," Roland said walking behind her, looking into my eyes with a cold look on his face.

Mary led me to the living room and I apologized for abruptly leaving the house before they came back from lunch. I tried my best to compose myself and not let her know the fury which I felt inside me. "I did not want to overstay my welcome," I lied to her.

"Oh, honey, just as I said before, Land's friends are my friends. Besides, I haven't had a chance to embarrass him in front of you," she said, while she searched through some photo albums, which sat on the coffee table. "Wait until you see pictures of him when he was a little boy," she said pleased that I was back.

"Honey," she said, "Land told me that you are a collector?" She asked me with sweet questioning eyes.

I knew I was in trouble then.

"What is it that you collect?"

"She collects maps. Maps and coins," Roland said hastily, forcing me to agree with him.

"Yes," I told her looking at him, and I swallowed the knot in my throat that was making me sick. For now, I was playing his game.

It was not ok what he was doing to me. It was not ok what he was doing to the lady who absolutely thought the world of him.

"I am here because there is going to be an auction at the Ritz," I said and I looked at him in defiance, showing him that I could play his game.

"Oh . . . the Ritz again, we don't like it there do we Land?"

Mary walked into the kitchen, leaving me alone in the room with the stranger who was playing a dangerous game with me. It was a dangerous game for him to be playing, for I had nothing to lose anymore. The only one who could get hurt was he. There were absolutely no more places for scars in me.

Mary came back to the room carrying a tray with the chocolate mousse from the night before. This reminded me that I had not seen Roland since dinner, when he answered the call and told us that he was going to step out for a few minutes—but did not come back for hours. I had hoped not to see him again.

I was feeling ashamed playing his game. Inside me, there was a fury waiting to explode. I was just trying not to do it in front of Mary. After all, she seemed like a kind lady, but did she really know her Land?

Roland ate his mousse while Mary insisted on showing me some old family pictures. She kept the albums like treasures, for they held the accounts of her Land's life.

I vaguely remember the pictures, but there were pictures of Land steering grandpa's boat; Land riding his bike; Land in his school play; Land blowing out ten candles; Land, Mary, Grandpa and Douglas.

Douglas?

I turned the page of the old yellowed album back and tried to focus on the picture where Roland was standing next to him. I could not believe my eyes. My heart sank, and together all my dreams sank with it. Who was Roland? Why was he in a picture with Douglas?

It could not be. I looked at Roland and tears filled my eyes. He grabbed me by the hand and dragged me out the door, giving Mary some excuse, which I could not comprehend; my brain had detached from my heart and all reason had vanished.

He pushed me inside the elevator, which felt claustrophobic, and he closed the iron door behind us. The sound of the old metal door being slammed was terrifying. As I watched the floors through the elaborate iron door as we descended in the old building, I felt as if I was going to throw up. I was light headed and my knees were going to give up on me. My heart started to race as he tightened his grip. It was the same feeling from the day before, while flying from Morocco next to him.

I obeyed him and followed him out of the elevator and out through the huge iron doors which guarded his home. I tried to take a breath, but instead I choked on my tears as he pushed me against the building's wall where he held my other hand and pressed his body against mine. Now, he had both my hands and his face was inches from mine. I finally gave in. My knees gave in, and he pressed his body harder into mine so I would not fall to the hard ground. He let go of one of my hands and touched the back of my head. As he did so, my chin fell on his chest and I felt beaten. I did not know what to do.

Chapter 24

The Crime I Was Going to Commit, 1988

——————————————————————— Back in Brazil ———

I CALLED THE WITCHES' HOUSE but there was no answer. I left a message telling them that I was leaving the next day for Rio for my job interview and that I would try to call again soon. I hung up the phone inside the old phone booth and stood there for a moment. I knew then that I was going to do what Douglas had asked me. *But why?*

I walked back to my apartment and Douglas was there, sitting on the veranda waiting for me. We went over and over his plan since he wanted to make sure I knew exactly what to do, once I got in the monastery.

"This is the room where you will find the letter," he said, showing me the map of the building. "I know you can do it," he said, knowing that I was going to follow every step of the plan. We continued to go over and over the plan until he decided that I was ready.

When Douglas left in the early morning, I still had not packed. The sun was almost rising and the purple sky was giving in to the sunrays. The bus to Rio wasn't leaving until noon so I threw a couple of changes in my backpack and tried to rest a bit. It did not work. My mind was racing. I could not help but think about Douglas. He had trusted me with his madness, and now I wasn't sure what to make of him anymore. *Is he crazy? Really? No.* I thought.

I finally drifted to sleep and felt my soul rising to another dimension. From there, where my soul was, I watched my body laying on the bed and my life played out before my eyes.

First, there was my childhood—when the days seemed so long and so bright. Then, there was plenty of time to play, dream, and live in a fantasy, which only children can do. Then, there was my reality—the crime I had committed, and the crime I was going to commit. Slowly I let my soul descend back into my body. The air, which had been holding me, carefully put me back in place and as I came back to reality, there was pain, there was terror, and there was an instinct to run away. I fought the nausea in my stomach. I fought the pain in my heart and by noon I was ready to leave.

I knew what I had to do, and I was going to do it, but still, I was unsure of so much.

Chapter 25

Trinidad

I ARRIVED IN RIO DE JANEIRO the next morning, and Douglas' nephew, Rafael, was waiting for me by the bus terminal. I didn't notice him approaching me as I stepped out of the bus, and I looked around hoping to recognize him.

"Hello," I heard an Argentinean accent say.

I turned my face and saw him.

"Hi," I replied, pleased to see him, and happy to have someone waiting for me.

"Welcome to Rio," he said with a contagious smile.

"Thank you," I said sincerely.

"How is uncle doing?" Rafael asked me.

I told him that Douglas was doing well and that he was just waiting for his boat to be repaired, and back in the water, so he could continue with his trip.

I told Rafael the exact same story that Douglas had told me about the storm that had broken the *True North's* mast. By then, I didn't know if I believed it or not. I did tell Rafael that I was glad that it had happened; otherwise, I would not have met his uncle.

I followed Rafael to the parking lot where we got into his Jeep and he drove us away. It was a nice drive and I was amazed with the beauty of the city. The sun, rising behind the mountains, made the day dance in front of us, and the breeze in my face made me feel refreshed. I finally understood why Rio was called "*Cidade Maravilhosa*."

I was busy absorbing my surroundings when Rafael asked me, "How well do you know my uncle, Marina?"

That took me by surprise.

"Not too well." I said, then, after thinking for a second I corrected my answer.

"Maybe too well," I said, wondering.

"Has he ever mentioned his friend Magellan to you?" Rafael asked with a bit of sarcasm.

"As a matter of fact he has," I answered him surprised that he had asked me about it so boldly. "I must tell you that their friendship is quite fascinating," I told him, trying to sound as cynical as he did about the subject. Although I was trying to sound careless about it, it was hard to not let my anxiety surface. To me, what Douglas had proposed had become a delicate subject, and I really did not want to talk about it.

I didn't want to tell Rafael all I knew about Douglas' friend and about his uncle's theory, but Rafael kept on going.

"Uncle is crazy. He's always looking into some crazy stuff to keep him busy. It's almost as if he needs it to survive," Rafael said driving into a private harbor. "It feeds his madness," he told me parking alongside a big ship anchored at the Marina da Glória.

Rafael jumped out of the Jeep and ran around it to open the passenger door. I was glad we had arrived and was hoping that Rafael would not bring up Magellan again.

"Welcome home," he said, crossing the bridge to the magnificent boat in front of us.

It was breathtaking. The ship was big, striking, and it looked old. *Something out of Douglas' history books,* I thought.

"Cool, right?" said Rafael, from up on the ship, noticing how thunderstruck I was to be facing such beauty. He walked back to the Jeep and grabbed my backpack, and while carrying it onboard, he explained to me that the ship was a replica of the Old Portuguese caravels, which had landed on the coast of Brazil around the 1500's. On carved wood, the name *Trinidad* was branded to the bow. The name jumped out at me as I remembered it being the same name as the caravel commanded by Ferdinand Magellan on his last voyage.

I walked across the wood hanging bridge connecting the land to the ship and stepped aboard. Fifty feet long, with comfortable sleeping rooms, a kitchen and a dining room, a game room and a bar; all inside the old looking ship—there were the comforts of the modern world.

That was Rafael's home for the moment and it was there that I was going to be staying while in Rio.

Who is Rafael trying to fool? I thought, as I saw how in love he was with the ship and the sea.

He loved his uncle too. And, I bet that he accepted his uncle's theory about "his friend" Magellan. *He simply doesn't want to admit it.*

"Rafael sailed to Rio from Argentina," said Douglas, when he told me that he had contacted his nephew in Rio de Janeiro and that the nephew was going to take care of me while I was there.

"Rafael finished up his business degree and took off on his adventure," said Douglas. "He says that he is going back home next year to take over his dad's business," Douglas told me, "but guess what? There is no way in hell that the kid is going back home. At least, not in a year!" Douglas finished, satisfied.

Rafael was shorter than I. His light brown hair framed his face just fine. His smile was contagious. His gray-green eyes were sincere and transparent and that's why I, too, didn't think he would be going back to Argentina any time soon. Even though he sounded sure about it, his eyes betrayed him.

His skin had a light tan that complemented his face and his hazel hair. His body was toned, but not overdone. I noticed it when he took his t-shirt off as soon as he hit the deck of the *Trinidad*. His subtle toned body said a lot about him. He was busy—and he liked it that way.

Rafael showed me my room and told me that I was welcome to stay as long as I needed.

"My boss is in Bariloche," he told me. "He won't be back for a couple of days," and he sounded pleased that for now, he was the one in charge of the vessel.

"Uncle Douglas wants me to take good care of you," he teased me with a mischievous look in his eyes. "He likes you, and he told me not to mess around," he said flirting with me.

"And by the way, I will be your driver. Uncle wants me to keep an eye on you," and he smiled again impishly.

"Thank you Rafael," I said, while unpacking the few things I had brought with me.

"Uncle said that you have a job interview with the Royal Cruise," Rafael said sitting on the bed. "I thought about applying for the job too, but I can't leave this yet," and he opened his arms gesturing around us.

Yes, it was a nice life he was living aboard the *Trinidad*. I would not leave it either.

"My interview is tomorrow morning," I told him. "Here, I have the address," and I handed him the piece of paper where I had written the Royal Cruise's line address.

Rafael looked at the paper, and said that we would have to leave early if I wanted to make it on time for the interview.

"Traffic gets crazy in the morning," he said. "We are going to have to leave around seven, so we can stop for breakfast at *Casa Rosa*. They make the best breakfast in town."

"Are you sure you don't mind driving me Rafael? I can get a taxi."

"No way," he said, leaving the room.

"Get changed and come eat something . . . " I heard him saying as he walked away.

I changed into some shorts and a t-shirt and was leaving the room when a framed picture by the door caught my attention. It was an old and weathered piece of paper framed inside the smudged glass. It had a faded stained drawing on it, some sort of a map. I stared at it for a second and found myself thinking about what Douglas had asked me. *He is crazy!* I told myself. I shook the thought out of my mind and I walk out of the room and went around the *Trinidad* looking for Rafael. I found him on the deck with a tray full of crab legs.

"Fresh as can be," he said, showing me the tray and shoving a huge piece of crabmeat into his mouth.

I walked to him and joined in the feast. We talked for hours and I felt as if I had known Rafael all my life. When night came we lay on the deck of "his" boat until the breeze was cold enough to send us in and break the spell between us.

"Good night Rafael, and thank you for everything," I said, when we walked inside the boat.

"You are welcome *chica*," he said, with his Argentinean accent.

I walked to my suite and lay on the bed. There was a silence—only interrupted by the sound of the water underneath the boat. I stared at the old framed picture by the door and the boat's swaying rocked me to sleep. I woke up the next morning with Rafael knocking on my door telling me that if I didn't get up right away we would never make it in time for my interview.

"We have to beat the traffic, *chica*," he said and he opened the door and handed me a cup of coffee.

I dressed in the clothes I had carefully picked out for the interview and looked at myself in the mirror. *OK,* I said. *I can do this!* And I walked outside onto the deck and found that Rafael was already in the car waiting for me.

Rafael drove us through the busy streets of Rio de Janeiro

until he parked in front of an old colonial building with a sign hanging over the door that said: *Casa Rosa*.

The breakfast was as good as Rafael had told me. He ordered us his favorite French bread sandwich, and we finished it in less time than it took for us to sit down and order. In less than twenty minutes we were out the door and on our way to my interview.

The office of the cruise line was tucked inside the ground floor of a two-story building in downtown Rio. I stepped into the waiting room where people were already waiting impatiently for their interview, and I felt the heat. I sat on the only brown vinyl chair left empty and thought about Rafael waiting for me outside.

"Good luck *chica*, and no worries. You are getting on that ship!" he assured me when I got out of the car, but still, his encouragement did not ease my anxiety.

Chapter 26

Vinyl Chair

WHEN I STEPPED OUT of the stuffy room, with walls covered in filing shelves, where I had been interviewed, I was dripping sweat. It seemed to me that I had been in there, cramped in that cubicle, for an eternity. I sat on the same vinyl chair where I had been sitting earlier and tried to catch my breath—praying, hoping to get hired. The interviewers had told me that I had to be back at four o'clock to find out if I got the job or not. It was done. Now, I just had to wait for the verdict.

I walked out of the building and Rafael was still sitting in his car. He jumped out as soon as he saw me, and went around and opened the passenger door for me. His bright, and mischievous smile comforted me, making me feel calm. I told him that I would have to be back later to know if I got the job.

"*Chica*, who will say no to you?" he said, with an optimism that I envied. "Of course they will hire you!"

I wondered if Rafael was always in such high spirits. He made me feel good.

"Let's go," he said. "I will take you to the most spectacular place you've ever been," and he turned the key on inside the Jeep. "We will be back here by four."

Rafael took me to see the statue of Jesus, at the famous Corcovado Mountain. It was just like he had said, "the most spectacular place." We drove to the top of the hill, where the huge statue took the city's breath away. It was majestic! I had seen pictures of it before, but being there was an incredible experience. The statue was so powerful, so omnipotent that it made the city underneath look like it was kneeling at his feet.

The statue of Jesus with his arms wide open was telling me, "Come. Come to me and I will protect you."

It was an overwhelming experience. I cried and I prayed. I prayed for the beauty of the scenery, I prayed for my life, I prayed that I would be hired and I gave thanks for all I had been through—for I knew that it was his way.

At four o'clock, I was back again, sitting on the brown vinyl chair in the hot waiting room. The room was full of us—waiting to be sentenced.

"God, I hope I get on that ship . . . " I prayed again.

I was the last one to be called in, and I was nervous because I had seen a few people coming out of the room with defeated looks on their faces. When my name was called I could barely stand on my feet. *God, I want it so much.*

I managed to drag myself into the room where I could not breathe, and then, I was sentenced to report to the ship in twelve days. Twelve days until my new life! I could not believe it.

Hyperventilating, I walked out of the building and saw Rafael lounging in his Jeep. One look at my face, and he jumped out of the automobile and grabbed me in his arms.

"I told you *chica*. You are on that ship! Nobody would say no to you."

His hug felt so comforting, that I did not want to let go of him. His aura, his smile, who he was; he was perfect! But when I told him that I was leaving that night to go back to Canasvieiras, he was shocked.

"*Chica*, you don't have to rush. You have two weeks." He tried to convince me.

"No Rafael. I have to be back here in twelve days and I have so much to do at home before I leave," I lied.

No, I did not have much to do. I just wanted to run away from Rio. Run away from the city where the monastery sat, supposedly holding the letter Ferdinand Magellan wrote to his wife. I could not grasp the fact that if I stayed, I would actually steal it for Douglas.

I stuffed the few changes of clothes I had onboard the *Trinidad* back in my backpack, rushing to get out of there. I felt that if I stayed a minute longer I would become a thief. I walked out of the caravel and Rafael drove me to the bus station.

That night, sitting inside the bus on my way back to the Island of Florianópolis I was feeling distressed because I didn't go through with Douglas' plan. But how could I? I wasn't a thief.

But, if it is true what Douglas told me about Magellan, then, someone is hiding something from the world. Can it be possible? How did I get involved in this?

"Uncle is crazy," I remember Rafael saying, not too convincingly.

Now, after meeting Rafael, I felt that I was a little closer to Douglas than I had been, but still, I did not steal for him. Not at that time.

In the bus, on my way back to the Island, I dreamed about the warm bread coming out of the clay oven back at the bakery where I worked as a teenager. I dreamed about the dirt road by grandma's fort where I used to cover myself in red dirt. I dreamed about the chickens . . . and then, there were his words: "You go get what you want," Lucien told me when I lay in his arms, the night I became a woman. It had sounded so sweet. And I dreamed about the bullets coming out of the barrel. Bang, bang, and bang. I gasped for air.

I slept and I dreamed about all those things, but dreaming about the closet was suffocating. I gasped for air again and when I woke up I cried in silence.

I can't breathe. I need fresh air. I walked to the front of the bus where the driver's cabin was and I asked her if I could keep her company. The driver showed me the empty seat close to hers and told me that I had to go back to my own seat before we arrive in the next town, otherwise she could get in trouble. I thanked her and closed the door behind me, separating us from the rest of the bus.

The window by her side was open, letting the cool breeze of the night blow through. The air felt good on my face and it kept me awake. I didn't want to fall asleep; I was afraid I would dream again.

It was a pleasant ride, talking to *Senhora* Amélia— the driver. She told me about how she got into the driving business, and I told her all about my new job. I told her that the ship, which I was going to be working on, would be going to the coast of Portugal and to the Mediterranean Sea. She just nodded her head—she did not have a clue what I was talking about. But she was a really good listener.

I was so thrilled to be telling her all about my new job that I forgot about my bad dream, and just before we arrived in São Paulo, our first big stop, *Senhora* Amélia told me that I had to go back to my seat. She said goodbye, and wished me good luck—she had finished her work and was passing the bus on to another driver.

As she walked by the bus window where I was sitting, I opened the glass and waved at her. I would never see her again. She was a really good driver . . .

Nine more hours and I would be in Florianópolis.

Chapter 27

Telling Him

I arrived in Florianópolis exhausted. It had been only a few days without seeing Douglas, but the minute I walked into my little apartment he was knocking at my door. There he was, with his smile from ear to ear, and a look of anticipation on his face that made me break down to tears. I had failed him! And I had to tell him that.

Douglas seemed to not have understood what I told him. I was expecting him to be enraged, but instead, he just stood there looking at me with his square smile.

I was starting to explain why I didn't go through with his plan, and why I didn't steal the letter for him when he put his hand on my shoulder and walked me out of the veranda onto the beach.

"Shhh . . . I know . . . I know," he whispered, embracing my shoulder with his long arm, making me feel safe.

"I am sorry," he said. "I am sorry for ever asking you to do such a horrible thing," he pleaded me. "You're still young, with much to live for," he said, with regret in his eyes. "Forgive me. And forget about it." He told me, and we walked to the shore, where the fishing canoes were resting, and we sat on the sand to watch the sunset.

"So? Did you get the job?" he asked me kindly.

I nodded my head and he smiled. He was pleased. He wanted that for me.

That night, he cooked fish with banana, which he knew was my favorite, to celebrate my new job. He told me about the places I should go visit in Europe and he said that he was happy for me.

"See? Now you will see the world, and I know you are going to make the most of it," he assured me. He took his glasses off and rubbed his tired eyes.

I knew he was sad.

I was sad, too.

I did not want to leave him. He had become my bollard, my fort. And now, now I was going to leave him and only God knew if I would ever see him again.

That evening, when I got myself into bed, I was tired and confused. I did not expect Douglas to accept so easily the fact that I did not steal for him.

Chapter 28

An Address

THE DAY I LEFT FLORIANÓPOLIS, Douglas drove me to the airport and stood at the large glass window until the airplane lifted from the ground. I could see his silhouette diminishing as I vanished into the big sky. This time, I was the one leaving.

"No. Absolutely not! You will go by plane!" He said. "You have to rest before you start your job, otherwise you are going to be a wreck when you get on that ship," Douglas said, while I tried convincing him that I was going to be fine riding the bus.

As we walked inside the airport, he handed me a piece of paper with an address on it.

"Here," he said. "If you stay in Portugal long enough, pay a visit to my old friend João, will you?" he asked me, from behind his thick glasses. "João will show you a good time," Douglas told me, and I noticed his eyes drifting away, to a very distant past, where he and João had lived their golden years.

"Tell him that I'm still chasing it, and tell him that the day I put my hands on it, he will be the first to know." Douglas asked me, and I saw on his face the feeling of entitlement. He wanted it and felt entitled to it. It was just as I remembered him to be, back when he strutted down the old cobblestone road, in my old city where angels sang over the church's bell, as if he owned it.

The paper he gave me had his almost illegible writing on it. It read:

João Menezes.

Rua dos Correeiros, 1300 Lisboa, Portugal.

I kissed him goodbye and walked away leaving him standing by the window. I was already missing him, however, knowing that my new life waited for me inside some big ship docked in Rio de Janeiro made me somehow gather the strength I needed. Still, my heart was aching. Douglas had become part of my life, and now that he had found me, I was leaving him behind. I was leaving everything I knew, everything and everyone I loved.

I arrived in Rio in less than four hours, and I was amazed at how fast the plane took me there. I could not help but regret all the hours I had wasted on bus rides.

———————————— Back in Rio to depart on the cruise. ———

As I walked through the gate I saw Rafael waiting for me. We hugged and I thanked him for being there again.

"No problem *chica*. For you? I'd do anything, anytime." He was so gentle, so real.

When we got to the *Trinidad*, Rafael told me that he had sailed up North to Cabo Frio.

"We got some rough waters on the way there and the boss's wife said to turn back," Rafael told me, almost laughing. "That was it for her. She said that she had had enough of water. She told my boss that if he wanted to play pirate he could do it on his own, but she was through with it. You should have seen it. She left screaming and cussing at the *Trinidad*. Can you believe it?" He asked sounding offended that someone would ever want to leave that ship. "I don't think they are coming back for a while *chica*. So make yourself at home," he told me as if he owned the ship.

It felt good to be with Rafael and on the *Trinidad* again, and I made myself at home just like he had offered. I went down to my room and changed into some comfortable clothes, and marveled at the ship. It was pristine. The caramel colored interiors were welcoming and warm, and all the brass glittered. On the bed there was a t-shirt that said Brazil on it, and a note from Rafael saying that it was for me to remind me of home while I was away. How sweet. I put on my new t-shirt and I was walking out of the room when I was distracted again, by the old faded map, framed by the door. I smiled at it thinking of Douglas and the many maps he had shown me in the last months. Yes, I was going to miss him.

I walked out of the room and met Rafael on the deck where he was busy polishing some instruments he used to sail. It felt good to just sit by him and marvel at the harbor.

That night, we lay on the deck until the breeze tried to send us away, but instead, we got some blankets and we cuddled up to each other. When I woke up the next morning,

Rafael was still asleep next to me and the first rays of the sun were lighting the day. I sat there and watched him for a while. His freedom was contagious. It would be nice to stay, but no, I was going to leave him too.

The Marina da Glória where the *Trinidad* was berthed was majestic. From there I could see the striking Pão de Açúcar peak, emerging from the town. Far away, I could see the statue of Cristo Redentor, perched tall—blessing the city. That time of the day everything seemed still. Everything seemed calm. Rafael woke up and cuddled back with me. He pulled the blankets back on us, since the early breeze was still cool, and we fell back asleep. By the time we woke up again we were sweating under the blankets.

Rafael took me on a tour of Rio de Janeiro since the last time I came for the interview with the cruise line I ran away as soon as I could. Now, I had nowhere to go but to wait to get on the ship. Rio de Janeiro was wonderful, and Rafael and I had a couple of fun days relaxing in the *Trinidad*, and going around the city.

The day I left to board the *Queen Leonor*, Rafael was the one who was there saying goodbye to me. I pleaded with him to call his uncle and make sure to keep in touch with him.

"And be a good boy yourself," I told him, before I walked into the office where I was going to report for work.

"No worries *chica*, uncle will be fine, he always has been," Rafael told me, unconcerned.

"Next time you talk to him, please tell him that I will see him again," I begged Rafael.

"And me, *chica*? Will I see you again?" he asked me with a sincere look in his eyes.

I kissed him and he kissed me back. "Maybe," I said, and started to walk to the office with my bag hanging on my side.

Chapter 29

Portugal, 1991

I NEVER SAW RAFAEL AGAIN, and with Roland holding me against that cold wall I knew that I would never see anybody anymore.

Roland was in possession of the most valuable thing I had ever put my hands on, and God I wanted it back! But how? I felt so defeated.

"Beware," Douglas said once when we were sitting in my kitchen back at my little apartment in Canasvieras. "It is a crazy world out there." He advised me.

Now, with Roland's fierce eyes glued to mine, his harsh jaw almost touching my face, I suddenly recalled his grandmother telling me, "How can we say no to him, right?"

Roland pressed his body harder against mine, into the cold wall and told me to be quiet.

I listened, and my silence was just a confirmation of Mary's affirmation.

How is he going to kill me?

There is no closet to hide in.

I took a deep breath and Roland stepped back from me, letting go of my hands.

Chapter 30

Queen Leonor, 1988

WHEN I BOARDED THE SHIP I could hardly control my excitement. Just two weeks before, I was sitting on the brown vinyl chair in the stuffy waiting room of the Royal Cruise Line's office hoping to be hired. Now, here I was—on my way to my freedom. I was leaving Brazil on my only way out.

I quietly knocked on the door of the cabin to which I was assigned. My cabinmate opened the door and showed me a friendly smile.

"Hi," she said, looking at my small luggage sitting on the floor next to me.

"Hi," I replied walking inside the cabin placing my luggage on the narrow floor between us. "I am Marina," I told her and kissed her on the cheek. She looked pleased that I had arrived and she wasted no time making me feel comfortable.

"I'm Elisa. I hope you don't mind, but I guess this is my bed," she said frowning at the mess lying on the cot she had already assigned to herself. "Since I already put all my stuff on it," and she gave me a guilty smile.

Yes, we are going to be just fine!

Elisa was from the State of Bahia—all the way in the Northeast of Brazil, and she too was happy to be on the job. She seemed nice and sincere, but absolutely silly, which made me like her instantly. We unpacked our luggage while chatting about what we thought the job was going to be like, and the places we were going to see. She told me that her family owned a cacao plantation back home in Bahia, and that her boyfriend had recently broken up with her, inspiring her to apply for the job. As she mentioned the ex-boyfriend, she attempted to make a disdainful face. It did not work, the look made her look even more childish, making me laugh.

I finished putting my stuff away in the small compartment next to my bed and marveled at the mess, which still sat on Elisa's bed. There was no doubt that her belongings were not going to fit in her small closet, and I was waiting for the moment she was going to attack the spare room in mine.

When we left our cabin to report to the Atlantic Room where we were having a crew meeting, our room was still only half organized—thanks to my new roommate.

When we arrived, the room was already full with the new crew. Everyone was happy and excited but as the officers entered the area, we all quieted down. The meeting was short and to the point. We were instructed on the safety procedures, and were told to show respect to passengers and to each other, but we were also reminded that we were the lucky ones to make it onto the cruise. The officers told us that we were expected to work hard, but to not forget to have some fun while doing it.

"Remember, this will be your home at sea, and this is your

family now, so please count on each other to make life easier," the captain said, raising an eyebrow at us.

The new crew was divided into groups, and we were given a training schedule for the week that we would be crossing the Atlantic. I was going to work at the pool bar, and Elisa was going to be in one of the dining rooms. They told us to report to our designated areas the next morning and excused us to go explore the ship until dinnertime when we were going to meet the ship's Chef.

My cabinmate and I walked around the ship and we realized how enormous it really was when we got ourselves lost and needed to follow the directions posted on the walls to find the way back to our cabin. We came to the conclusion that the ship was more like a labyrinth than a home.

Back in the cabin Elisa attempted to organize the rest of her belongings, but without any luck. There was simply not enough space for it all, so I offered her the bottom of my closet.

At dinner, we all met again at the Atlantic Dining Room, where we were served an amazing meal prepared by the cruise's Chef. It was a celebration meal to welcome us on board, and halfway through, Jean, who was introduced to us as the Chef, gave us a speech.

"The passengers are always right," he said, resting his hands on his hips. "Never, ever, argue with them," he told us. "You are to keep your composure at all times. If you are bringing a dish back into my kitchen for any reason whatsoever, you better bring it with finesse. No one, no one is to notice it," and

Jean gave a look to us that said we had better listen to him. "You are expected to work and people are not supposed to see you until they look for you. Class and finesse, people, class and finesse! And please, don't forget, this is the Royal Cruise Line, and you are onboard the *Queen Leonor,* our passengers are all royalty." and Jean rolled his eyes as if in disbelief of his own words.

Jean was obsessive about his job. That much I could tell. I also could tell that he was capable of making one's life a living hell if things did not go his way. *Better be on his good side,* I thought, smiling to him. By the time dinner was over and the Chef had finished his performance, I was ready to fall into bed. Elisa and I walked back to our cabin following the directions on the wall and as I lay on the small bed on my new home, I felt my heart tightening. It was too much to take in. So many mixed feelings—a new job, a new life—leaving Douglas, leaving home.

I was on my way to the Old World!

My life had turned upside-down, and I felt guilty leaving Douglas behind. As I stared at the ceiling trying to fall asleep I could not shake him out of my mind. *Why didn't I steal the damn thing for him?* My remorse questioned me and I drifted away into wild dreams.

Chapter 31

Royalty

IT TOOK US LESS THAN TEN DAYS to get to Europe and it was enough time for me to reflect on my life and realize that I could not have done anything differently. I had to move on and I could not let my despair interfere with my destiny. So, slowly, I started to enjoy my new life and forget about my troubles. By the time the first passengers boarded my new home at the Port of Lisbon, I was feeling at ease in my new skin and was accepting the fact that I was going to live my life with no regrets. After all, there was nothing else to lose.

Without noticing, my nightmares had subsided, and the emptiness I felt was fulfilled by the busy life I was living on the ship. I was giving myself a chance to not be disturbed by my troubles and my nightmares and it was working. At least, for the time being.

I enjoyed the job and the crew, and the incredible cama-raderie among us; we had all left Brazil for the same reason. The money was good, and the cruise was our way to get out and see the world.

Elisa, my cabinmate, hers, was a different story. As I said, she came from a rich family up North in Brazil, and their cacao plantation, the source of her wealth, went way back in her family tree. The plantation was traced to the time when the Africans were brought to Brazil as slaves, and that made me tease Elisa telling her that her money was dirty money, and that it was made from the sweat of our African brothers. She used to get so mad that she would walk out of the cabin slamming the door, just to come back in seconds later, telling me that I was right.

I liked Elisa. She was fun, and easy to be with, but I was happy that our work schedules were different from each other, giving us each some time alone.

Now, with every stop we made, the passengers who came off and on the ship were amusing—they made work exciting. Some were eager to share their lives with the pool waitress, while others posed on the loungers as if they were real royalty, snapping their fingers when they wanted me to refill whatever drink they were binging on. The ones who wanted to share their lives with me told me secrets, which they should not have, and the ones who snapped their fingers, they drank much more than they should. The stories that some of them told me were callous, and I tried to forget them as soon as they spilled out. But these were the same passengers that when they left the ship they hugged me goodbye and told me to take care of myself, so I learned to listen to them with affection, if not respect.

Yes, it was a great cruise—and indeed, they were all royalty.

Chapter 32

Cádiz, Spain

I HAD BEEN ON BOARD the *Queen Leonor* for two months, and had stopped in beautiful places in Portugal, Spain, and France, when one morning, I realized that we were anchored at the port of Cádiz. I remembered that Douglas had mentioned the place numerous times throughout our lessons, back in my little kitchen in Brazil, so I decided to get off the boat and explore the place.

I ventured alone, since Elisa was working, and my new Portuguese friend Carla, who worked by the pool with me, had seen it "one too many times."

I walked away from the port and took a taxi to Playa de la Calleta—one of the places Carla had recommended. It was early morning, and the sunlight on the town's rooftops was reflecting the town's past. In the European guide that Rafael had given me, before I left Rio, it said that Cádiz was more than three thousand years old, and that it had survived the rise and fall of Phoenicians, Carthaginians, Moors and Romans. *What happened?* I asked myself. *How did I end up here?* I inhaled the cool, fresh, moist air and immersed myself in the history of the Old Spanish place.

On the faces of its inhabitants, stillness reigned—they

emanated peace. Old couples walking by the sea, hand in hand, displayed a wisdom that I envied. It was a place that had survived ancient wars, but that still looked serene. Contrasting with the mixed, exotic architecture that sat behind my back, the bright beach was crowded with people. Children, families and young couples tanning in the sun—hugging the sand— were making me jealous. The colorful beach umbrellas gave the place a cheerful feel, while at the sand's edge the ocean at the Spanish feet remained calm. I sat on its fine white sand and contemplated the scenery for a while, and then I ventured into town.

Cádiz was a vibrant town where people strolled carelessly on its old colorful streets giving it an exhilarating character. Beautiful loud people, sitting on their esplanades, sipping their cafés and savoring the sun, made me want to join them. Although I had never been here before, the place felt familiar to me, and finding myself in the midst of a world that I had imagined so many times, but never really believed could be real, made me feel a little closer to Douglas.

I entered a café with the name of *Santa Maria* painted in bright red and yellow colors above the door, and was greeted by a friendly waitress. Although most were drinking coffee I ordered a glass of juice and sat on the esplanade by myself. It felt awkward sitting there alone, so I was glad to have my guidebook, other than people watching, to keep me busy. I wished Elisa had been off work too, since I knew she would have joined me. I drank my juice and was ready to leave when the people sitting next to me started to make small talk.

Between my Portuguese, and their Spanish, we managed to have a conversation. They introduced themselves as Cristina and Agustín. They were cousins, and they had come to their grandparent's home for the summer. They told me that they had grown up in Cádiz, but were going to university in Seville, which they told me was not too far from there. I told them that I was going to be in town for one more day, and then, the cruise would continue on the Mediterranean Sea. I drank another juice, while they sipped coffee, and smoked cigarettes.

"I have to get going," I said, not making any effort to leave, because I was enjoying being with them at the esplanade. It felt as if I was starting to fit in. They were so friendly, that after a half an hour talking at the café, it seemed to me that I had known them my whole life.

"Marina, come to Grandpa's house tonight, we will have dinner together, OK?" said Agustín, and he wrote a phone number on a napkin and gave it to me.

"Please come," said Cristina, his cousin. "Call us and we'll come get you," she told me with a smile.

I stood up, and kissed their cheeks to say goodbye. I walked inside the café to pay my bill, putting the napkin with their phone number inside my wallet. I did not think I could make it to dinner since I had to work that evening, but I kept the number anyway.

As I was leaving the café, a familiar portrait grabbed my attention and I walked to the wall where the picture was hanging. It was framed in an old, golden frame. I had seen him before, the man depicted on it. He was robust, with heavy features, and his beard was black and full. I read the words beneath it: "The world was his."

What a coincidence, I thought, to see that picture on the café's wall. It was the same picture, which Douglas had shown me in my small kitchen back at my apartment on the beach of Canasvieiras. It was a picture of the man Douglas was fascinated about. It was Magellan.

At first, it was just a picture on a wall in a café. But later, it became a ghost to me. As I walked the streets of Cádiz back to the ship, I kept remembering the man in the picture, and thinking of what Douglas had confided to me.

Could Douglas be right?

Was everything really lost, or was there more to know about Magellan?

Maybe I should have done what Douglas had asked me. No! I am not a thief. I could not have done it. But then I remembered that I was a murderer.

Chapter 33

Casa Blanca In Cádiz

WORK THAT EVENING WAS EASY since most passengers chose to stay on land. Still, I felt stuck on the ship after my amazing day in town. I finished my shift earlier than I was scheduled to, and walked to my cabin where I found Elisa relaxing in her bed, reading a book. I had a hot shower and was putting my sleep t-shirt on when I changed my mind.

"I am out of here," I told Elisa, and started to change into my jeans.

"I'm coming with you," she said, jumping out of bed.

We walked off the ship and found a phone booth, where I called Cristina and Agustín.

"No," I said, when they asked me if we needed a ride. "We will get a taxi."

"Tell the driver to take you to the *Casa Blanca* in the *bahía*," Agustín said, and I asked him for directions.

"That's it. That is the direction." He paused. "Don't worry," he assured me. "The driver will know where it is."

We stood by the taxi stop for a few minutes and a cab stopped for us. We got in, and I told the driver what Agustín had told me. The man smiled.

"*Ah, van a la casa del Señor Antúnez?*" He asked us, which made me wonder if he had heard the direction I gave him.

"*Casa Blanca* in the *bahía, por favor,*" I repeated.

"Oh yes. *Señor* Antúnez house!" The driver confirmed.

We did not know where we were going, but it seemed that our taxi driver knew exactly where to take us. He drove us through the streets of Cádiz for a few minutes, and then, he stopped the vehicle in front of a big white cement wall. *Well, this must be the place,* I thought. We paid for the ride and got out of the cab. By the time we looked around, the taxi had already gone, so Elisa and I found ourselves standing by the gate quite unsure of what to do.

All we could see were the words: *Casa Blanca,* written in small calligraphic letters on a bronze plaque on the massive white wall, through which a narrow wood gate cut. There was no sign of anyone. No sight of a bell or any way for us to announce that we had arrived, so we bravely walked through the gate in the middle of the thick wall, under a natural arch made of bougainvilleas.

Lanterns lit the path toward a narrow stairway, which led to a carved wood door. The door was half open and as we climbed the rough cement stairs, we started to hear voices and the sounds of music coming from behind the mysterious walls. I pushed the door open and peeked inside. I did not believe my eyes. There, behind the intimidating white clay wall, people were dancing on the large veranda overlooking the sea. There were old people, young people, children, and even a lazy dog lying on the floor next to a clay planter, where a coconut tree was growing. We were standing by the door, digesting the scene, when Cristina saw us from across the area and waved us in.

"Come, come," she said, and she walked to us grabbing me by the hand and brought us over to join the comfortable crowd. Agustín, who was inside the large living room, came out of the house when he saw us.

"*Hola* Marina, I am glad you are here!" and he kissed my cheek and I introduced Elisa to him.

"*Hola* Elisa, welcome.

"Grandpa, this is Marina—the Brazilian girl I told you about," Cristina told the old man, who was sitting on a rocking chair playing a small four-string acoustic guitar. The soothing musical notes ceased and the old man stood up from his rocking chair, and walked towards us. He kissed my face, and held my hand in his for a while.

"Welcome!" He said, and he grabbed Elisa to receive his kiss.

The old man was charming. He sported perfectly groomed silver hair, and wore casual, but tailored clothes. On his face, a mustache did not interfere with his kind features, and the smile he gave to his wife when he introduced us to her showed me how much he loved her.

The scene suffused my senses, and I didn't believe that it was real.

Do these people live like this everyday? I could not help but wonder.

The veranda was covered with bougainvilleas, which also

covered the entry gate. Dark, natural wood trellises held the flowers above our heads. Oiled wood chairs and sofas, covered with purple colored pillows, were scattered around the veranda, giving everyone a place to rest. A big table that held more seats than I could count sat at the far right end of the veranda, where I could see the vast sky. A barbecue built into the brick wall was slowly cooking the sausages, which smelled so delicious. The Grandpa gave us each a plate with the sausages and garnished it with fresh warm bread. Oh, it was heavenly! Cristina poured us some drink, which she made with white wine and citrus soda, and the crowd saluted us. The drink was refreshing and sweet, with just the right amount of alcohol in it, and the people were making us feel welcome.

We sat on the veranda under the Spanish sky and chattered about everything one could possibly imagine, but what kept Cristina and Agustín's Grandpa most excited, was talking about how the Portuguese had colonized Brazil instead of the Spanish, and the spectacular Brazilian soccer players, with their recent million dollar contracts with European soccer clubs. We talked about Ayrton Senna, the great Brazilian Formula One racer, whom Cristina believed was going to cause her grandfather to have a heart attack one day.

"Grandpa loves Senna," Agustín told us.

"Who doesn't?" asked the Grandpa, adding that he had never seen anyone drive so fast and so well in his entire life.

"Yes. We love Senna." I agreed with the old man, implying that Senna was the king of the Brazilians.

They asked about Carnaval, and I told them that it was a big part of our culture.

"We watch it on television," Cristina said.

"I want to go to Carnaval one day," Agustín told me excited. "I want to see it live!" and he tried to do a *samba* move, which looked to me more like a bullfighter's dance.

The family asked us about life on the ship. They asked us about life in Brazil. They were amazed by the Brazilian culture, and I felt at ease answering all the questions they had. And when the Grandpa started to talk about how the Spanish and the Portuguese had colonized South America, I realized how lucky I was to have met Douglas, and how lucky I was to have learned the lessons he taught me.

Douglas had opened a door through which I was making my way, and because of him, I sat there, fascinated by *Señor* Antúnez's stories about how the Spanish and the Portuguese had fought, trying to prove to one another that one was better than the other. Time flew by and I didn't want the night to end—contrary to my friend Elisa, who was falling asleep on the sofa next to the wood table, where Cristina, Agustín and I kept listening to their Grandpa's amazing stories. There I was, once again, being taken into an unimaginable world, where Douglas had taken me before. Suddenly I realized that it wasn't so far fetched anymore.

The night was long and somehow *Señor* Antúnez managed to keep grilling sausages, and Agustín kept filling my cup with *claro*. It was late when I realized that we had to get back to the ship. I got up from the chair where I was sitting across from Agustín, and turned to the house behind me. It was then that I saw a painting, which took up a good part of their living room wall. It was a painting of a boat.

Grandpa could see that I was intrigued, so he stood up and gallantly took me inside to show it to me.

"The greatest expedition of our time," he said, stopping in front of the painting, where a small gold engraved plaque on the frame read, "We made it around the world in three years and seven months, thanks to our Lord, Ferdinand Magellan."

Reading the small letters on the plaque made me dizzy and my knees almost gave out on me. I asked to use the washroom and *Señor* Antúnez showed me the way. I walked in and closed the bathroom door behind me and rested my shivering body against it.

Oh no, I am going to throw-up . . .

I splashed cold water on my face and fixed my hair back into a bun, and realized that I could barely stand. It was too much to take in—that Douglas could be right.

I have to open the door, I remember thinking.

And why, God? Why is this happening to me?

I had a vague memory of Douglas saying, "On the back of the letter is a map which Magellan drew, and the key to the map is in his words to his wife." After that, I don't remember anything.

That night, Elisa and I slept on the sofas of Cristina and Agustín's Grandpa's veranda, and when I woke up the next morning, my mouth was dry, and a hangover had over taken me. I managed to pry my eyes open and prop myself up against the back of the sofa thinking that we had to get back to the ship.

I got up slowly and walked to the edge of the veranda where I was stunned by the view. The house was sitting on the beach, and below, the Spanish ocean was calmly touching the rocky wall. I hadn't realized the night before that we were so close to the water.

Señor Antúnez's house was the last house on the *bahía* and the back of the house, where the veranda sat, faced the sea. I realized then, that I was getting accustomed to looking at the horizon and seeing only water.

What happened to the little girl running up and down the road covering her body with red dirt? Not in my wildest dreams . . . I thought.

We drank the strong coffee, which Mrs. Isabel had brewed, and Elisa and I were on our way back to the ship. I did not have the opportunity to say goodbye to my new friends' Grandpa since he had awoken before us and had gone fishing on his sea.

"He does it every morning," Cristina said. "Sometimes he just sits in his boat with his old friends and they stare at the ocean all day long," Cristina told me. "Not that he is crazy or anything like that," she added. "He just loves it."

We said goodbye to Mrs. Isabel, and I promised to call when the cruise ship returned to town. We jumped in Agustín's car and he and Cristina drove us back to the port.

That evening, after I finished working, I was still feeling slightly sick. I thought that it was the effect of too much *claro*, but by the time the ship lifted anchor, I was feverish and in bed.

I don't remember much of my illness, but I do remember Jean, the cruise's Chef, waking me up every so often and feeding me some kind of broth.

Chapter 34

Waiting to Die. Portugal, 1991

He stood in front of me and I felt defeated. My arms were limp, and I felt useless. He was going to kill me right there. BANG. One shot. Right in the chest! I closed my eyes and waited. Nothing. I squeezed my eyes tight and waited. Again, nothing. There was silence, and I had the impression that he had stepped away from me. I opened my eyes; not confident that I would find him, but instead, I saw him standing inches from my face and I was breathing his air. He had betrayed me, he was hurting me, and somehow, there were still places in my heart for a couple more scars. I wanted to fall into his arms. How could that be? He had stolen from me. He was going to kill me. I felt so vulnerable. I just wanted an arm to hold me while I died. And that's when he rescued me from my trance.

"Marina, listen. I am not going to hurt you. Listen to me Marina," Roland kept saying while he stood too close to my crushed being. My back, cold and hard against the wall, did not feel like enough to keep me upright.

I lowered my eyes to the ground. I didn't want to see his victory. *Who is he?*

"Listen Marina," he said again, making me aware of his

overwhelming presence. "I can't let you do this." He said not making sense. "It means too much to me. What will happen if the truth is exposed?" He asked me, still not making sense.

All I wanted was for him to give me back what was mine, and disappear from my life. I didn't think my stuff was worth any money.

He can't let me do this? It means too much for him? The truth can't be exposed? What does he mean by that?

Roland grabbed my hands, which were hanging limply by my sides, but this time his hands felt like ice—not the warm hand I felt on the flight from Casablanca. I tried to gain them back but it was useless. He dragged me away from the cold, sharp wall, where my back was taking refuge, and heartlessly dragged me across the busy street, and shoved me into his Citroën. I did not think to run. Nothing was making sense.

Chapter 35

Delirious

JEAN, THE CHEF, became my best friend. Even though we argued most of the time, I just could not stay mad at him. He was the one who cared for me while my body was burning up with fever and I became delirious.

"Cherie," he said, when I opened my eyes after the fever broke. "We need to talk."

Am I in trouble? I wondered.

Elisa came to visit me and said that she could barely wait to get back to our cabin—she didn't like her temporary cabinmate. She also said that Jean had been taking care of me since the night I got sick.

"When was that?" I asked her, not sure of how long I had been sick.

"The night after we stayed at *Señor* Antúnez's house." She said, as if I should have known it. "After that," she continued, "you became delirious, girl. Delirious!" and she shook her head, as if I should have known that too.

Elisa said that Jean got into a fight with the cruise's nurse, because the nurse didn't want him to be close to me. "She was afraid that Jean would get ill and make the whole ship sick. You should have seen it, girl." Elisa told me making fun of the

Chef. "You know how Jean can throw hissy fits if he doesn't get things his way," and she smiled, "but I never, ever, thought he could be such a ferocious man." She finished, still laughing at Jean's bold attitude.

"Delirious, Elisa? Come on!" I said, still feeling weak and barely able to sit up in bed.

"Yes girl. You were out of it!" and she looked at me with inquisitive eyes. "Jean said that you were so delirious, that you needed to see a psychiatrist or something. He said you are crazy!" Elisa dished it out, and said goodbye, leaving me speechless, stuck to my cot.

I lay there and tried to figure out what she meant by me being crazy. *Was I really that sick?* And I wondered what Jean wanted to talk about. I became anxious thinking that I was going to be sent home. *God, no. Please?* And in that hopeless state, I fell asleep again.

I had just woken up and was lying there in my little cabin, in that big ship, when Jean entered the room. My eyes were open, but I closed them as soon as they met his. I was terrified. I didn't want to lose my job, but for all I knew, chances were, I was going to be shipped off back to Brazil.

"Marina," he said, as he sat down next to me in bed. Jean held my hand, and I reluctantly opened my eyes. I was still weak. Weak from being in bed, weak from barely eating, and my heart was aching because I knew I was going to be rudely awakened from my dream. At least Jean was being compassionate, holding my hand, before telling me that I had to go.

"Hundreds of passengers come on and off this ship,

Marina," he told me. "We are lucky none of them got sick," and his grip tightened. "That cold nurse of ours was trying to get you off this boat!" he added, with a stubborn look. "I am glad you are all better, cherie. How boring it would be, without you here?" and he smiled. "I don't think I could survive."

The adrenaline was working its way through my body and I was confused by Jean's kindness. I lay in the cot, waiting for the bad news to come, but instead, Jean kissed my forehead and told me to get up and shower.

"You need to get some fresh air, cherie. Meet me by the pool when you are ready," and he walked out leaving me puzzled.

I managed to get in the shower and change into some fresh clothes. I made my way through the ship's passages, but felt dizzy walking on the pool deck, where Jean was sitting by the bar waiting for me with a drink. He ordered me to drink the concoction and I did it without arguing.

"Thank you Jean. Thank you for taking care of me." I said honestly.

I wasn't ready for what Jean said next, and so, I felt sick again.

"What is your problem with Ferdinand Magellan, and who the hell is Douglas?" he asked me boldly. "And by the way, cherie, just so you know," he continued, "you are not losing your job."

I tried to catch my breath and attempted to say something but I couldn't make a sound. I felt my head spinning, and for the first time, I thought that I was feeling seasick. *Why is he asking me these questions?*

"Go ahead cherie, I am listening." and he lit a cigarette, and sipped his green drink.

I stared at him. I wished I could run, but my weakened body could only sit there, in front of him feeling worthless.

"Come on cherie." He challenged me again.

"What are you talking about?" I finally asked.

He looked at me with inquiring eyes and said, "Do you know how many times you muttered the name of Magellan in your delirium? And this Douglas, who is he?"

I looked at Jean and realized that there was no need to hide anything from him, and so I told him. I told him everything. Everything! From the sounds of the bullets, which were still ringing in my ears, to the first lessons Douglas had taught me. I told him about the Jesuits in Rio de Janeiro, and I told him about Douglas's nephew Rafael. I told him about the café in Cádiz with the words on the wall where I first became aware that perhaps Douglas could be right. I told him about the *Casa Blanca* by the bay in Cádiz, where the picture on Christina and Agustín's Grandpa's wall—Magellan's Caravel—was clearly depicted. I told him about what Douglas had proposed that I do, and I told him that I wasn't a thief and that was why I didn't steal the dammed thing. As I poured out my troubled life, I saw Jean's eyes brightening. There was a glow that I had not seen on his face before. He looked more than alive; he looked ecstatic.

"I knew it!" his eyes were glimmering.

"I knew it!" He repeated.

"The French still think that they unraveled the world, and so do the Portuguese and the Spanish. Little do they know cherie, little do they know!" and with that, he walked to the bar—fetching a fresh drink.

"Yes, it makes sense," he said as he came back, "but it also could be a big delusion of this Douglas friend of yours cherie." Jean seemed to look at the situation from all angles. "If you pay attention to the explorer's maps, cherie, one can tell that they didn't have a clue where they were going. How many circles are there to find one place? How many circles does one explorer need to make before he finds what he is looking for?" He said with a bit of sarcasm, and continued, "I had an uncle who was fascinated by the navigators. He was a little crazy himself. My mother told me that he went sailing around the world looking for something. She loved her brother but she too thought that there was something wrong with him. He died in South America, and his boat; which had been his only possession, was left to my mother. Mom didn't want it so she let the thing sit there for too long, and when she died, I had to sell it to pay for the harbor fees. That thing was haunted. It was cursed!" Jean told me sadly. "I remember seeing my uncle once or twice, when he came to visit us in Biarritz. I was just a little boy and I was terrified by him. He looked scary!" Jean finished, and would never speak about him again.

I wasn't sure where he was going with all this, but I was puzzled by his knowledge on the subject and about the portrayal of his old uncle.

"Come on Jean, look at me." I said. "Until a year ago my world revolved around my own little troubled life," I said feeling ashamed. But Jean looked at me in ecstasy.

"What is the name of the town you lived in with your mother, cherie?" He asked out of the blue, and I reminded him.

"Paranaguá."

"*Voilà*! That's one of the places where Magellan anchored while sailing the coast of Brazil, cherie." he said, satisfied.

I felt a chill run through my body and had the feeling I was truly getting sick again. My heart started to beat faster and I felt panic.

"Jean," I pleaded him. "Stop it please!"

I was scared.

"It is not funny." I said, and tried to slow my respiration.

"No cherie," Jean said. "I am not kidding," and he continued, "I remember it from a documentary I watched about Magellan's around the world voyage," he said, more excited than ever. "When you told me the name of the town where you lived, I recalled hearing its name somewhere. It wasn't relevant then. But since your delirium, cherie, and all you are telling me, things are starting to make sense. Just look around, look where you are. Think about the things you just told me." Jean said, and then he paused, had a sip of his drink, took a long puff on his almost-gone cigarette, and stared at the horizon.

"Why did you apply for this job cherie? Why are all these coincidences happening to you? Believe me, it is deep inside you. If you could have heard yourself when you were sick, you would not doubt it. Your life is the one you get cherie, and *voilà*; this is your life. Don't walk away from it. Don't be afraid." he said, looking pleased that this was happening, and that he had become part of it.

"Imagine if what this Douglas told you is true. It could change history, cherie. Don't put yourself down don't make yourself sick. If the secret belongs to the world you are not stealing it, you are freeing it."

I couldn't breathe. *Why is this happening to me? Please stop.*

Instead of making me feel better, Jean's words were troubling me. It was all too surreal, like a dream, an awful wild dream.

"You only lose cherie, when you have something to lose." Jean said. "Look at you. Do you want to be serving drinks to bitches dressed in fake Gucci for the rest of your life? No, cherie! Go get it, make it happen."

The next day, when I was back working by the pool, Jean's words were echoing and unsettling my concentration. He was right. I looked at the faces around me, and there was nothing I wanted to surrender my life to, so I started to wonder if perhaps I should look for Douglas when I returned to Brazil. *Maybe I should have stolen the dammed thing.*

Chapter 36

Asking Forgiveness, 1991

As ROLAND DROVE US THROUGH the streets of Lisbon leaving the old, romantic buildings behind us, the tears, which had been confined to my eyes, began to trickle down my face. I felt salt on my lips and instantly I was taken back to the suffocating closet in my old house next door to the witches. The more the tears moistened my lips, the more distant and detached I felt and the more I cried. I cried for losing my mother, I cried for losing Douglas. I cried remembering the afternoon I spent on Cristina and Agustín's Grandpa's veranda facing their sea, and I cried for my witches who would never be free. Crying, I tasted the tears that poured down my face as I kissed my witches goodbye, the day I left them behind. I cried remembering Douglas asking me if I knew how to clean the fish that I was holding by its tail, back at the white sand beach of Canasvieiras. And, when I recalled the lessons, which he had so passionately taught me, the tears did not stop, and I remembered the Fortune Teller's words. Had she lied to me?

I deserve it, I told myself. *I deserve it all! But why?* Why did I think I deserved all that was happening to me?

I closed my eyes and recalled sitting on the wooden bench, listening to the old priest inside the monstrous, elaborate

Catholic Church, where pictures of a suffering Christ, shining from the massive stained glass windows, was supposed to make me feel guilty for my sins. There, where I used to sit through mass when I was only a girl, counting the minutes until I could get out of there, I remembered feeling hot and uncomfortable while listening to the priest's sermon, which was distant and unintelligible. But somehow, in the hot suffocating car, I remembered his words.

"Ask forgiveness for your sins, and you will be forgiven." Ask forgiveness . . .

Forgive me father for I have sinned.

*   *   *

I couldn't tell where the car was taking us, but I knew Lisbon was becoming remote. We drove past the famous Estoril beach and out of Cascais town, and I could see in the distance, the majestic Palácio da Pena, sitting atop the purplish green hills, above my divine Sintra. The fine rain falling on the car's window, kept me confused and unaware of where I was. I got glimpses of places I had seen before—but nothing was clear. My reason was gone. All was nebulous, as if a cloud had descended around me—not allowing me to see clearly.

Dusk was starting to play tricks, and more than an hour had passed, with me sitting next to Roland in the suffocating car, when we came to a stop in the cobblestone plaza. The plaza seemed familiar, but *no*, I'd never been there before.

I came to the conclusion that if Roland was going to kill me he was taking too long to do it, so I tried to focus on what had stopped us. I tried to become aware of my surroundings, but the raindrops falling on the vehicle's window kept the view unclear. Then, I saw him. It was a boy—slowly and precisely herding his sheep through town. Despite the darkening light, I could see the curious eyes of the young boy trying to identify us inside the stuffy car. His eyes found mine, and the look was similar to the look Lucien had given me, when I thought I was safe behind my Ray-Bans and the darkened windows of the Alfa Romeo, when I drove past his beach house, on my way to find Douglas. Just like Lucien, the boy saw through me, and yet, smiled. It was the most beautiful smile I had ever seen. His big white teeth, still too big for his face, but waiting to fit in, were perfect side by side. His tanned skin revealed a healthy, active child, kissed by the sun, and as he walked away from the plaza with his sheep surrounding him, I was finally able to breathe again.

I felt the dried tears on my face, and I felt free. As the car drove away from the plaza, I knew something really bad was going to happen, but I did not worry, nor did I care anymore. Then, we came to my final stop.

I got out of the car without fighting, and followed Roland to the entry gate where he was taking me. I had almost entered the yard when something grabbed my attention. *Casa do Carmo*, read the traditional blue and white Portuguese tile, affixed to the white cement wall. It startled me. With the anxiety and despair of being taken by Roland, and not knowing where I was being taken, I had simply let go of my reason, living in the sorrow prior to my murder. But, as I read those words, all of a sudden I felt grounded. *I have seen these words before!*

Casa do Carmo sat inside the walls of the picturesque city of Óbidos, where massive stone walls hold the history from times when Romans, Moors, and the Portuguese Empire ruled the country; history of a time when prejudice, mystery and despair lived side by side. And there, inside those walls, my history was being written.

The grand entry gate to the city, with the impressive tile art depicting the religion of the people that have prevailed in there, is a passage to the past. The cobblestoned streets, with narrow walkways, carry the weight of time, and, in every step, one is carried deep into the past, which was long ago, but pretends to be present. I remembered thinking that I had been there before, since the sign on the gate that said *Casa do Carmo* seemed so familiar. But no—I had never been there.

Chapter 37

The Chef

AFTER LEAVING THE PORT OF CÁDIZ and my new friends Cristina and Agustín, the illness took over my body. I was confined to the cabin where I learned later, that if it weren't for Jean, I would probably have been shipped off.

Jean nursed me back to health, but after, he made sure to turn what had been a mediocre life, into a living hell. He simply couldn't let go of the idea that a secret about Magellan had been bestowed upon me, and, as soon as we anchored in Barcelona, he arranged for us to go visit the city's *bibliotheca*.

I was terrified to leave the boat. I didn't want to find any support for Douglas hypothesis. But no, Jean was on a mission—to make my life impossible.

At the bibliotheca, he did not rest. He searched through old books, and old records, with a feverish eagerness that made me even more scared. He seemed possessed. He had to find something, anything, so he could prove to me that my illness hadn't been without meaning.

He asked questions, he took notes, and when we left empty handed, he was extremely disappointed. He couldn't understand how we could spend so much time, and walk away with nothing.

"*Rien*!" he said viciously, and left me as soon as we arrived back on board the *Queen Leonor*.

Good. I thought. *Now he will leave me alone*.

Little did I know about the Chef!

Jean kept researching Magellan's voyages, and, every little piece of information he found, he shared with me.

"Listen cherie," he said excited. "It says here that Magellan left the port of Seville on August 10, 1519."

"Yes. I know that." I told him.

"There were five ships in his expedition. Listen for their names cherie: *San Antonio, Concepción, Trinidad, Victoria and Santiago*." Jean looked at me with an exciting look in his eyes and asked, "What was the name of the caravel you stayed on, in Rio de Janeiro? Wasn't it *Trinidad*?" he confirmed. "See? No coincidence here cherie, it is destiny!"

Oh my God. How can he be so dramatic? I wondered.

Jean was becoming consumed with the idea that my friend Douglas wasn't crazy after all. He actually believed that there could be a secret waiting to be chased down and revealed. Now I not only had to deal with my demons, but Jean's devil as well.

He simply did not give up. In every port we stopped, he dragged me to libraries and museums, so that we could look for anything in compliance with Douglas's theories. Dreadfully, I followed him through his saga, and was thankful that all we found was an account of the time when Magellan's only surviving ship, the *Victoria*, had made it back to Spain, and the glorification of the men who survived with it.

I was getting tired, but Jean would not cease in his quest. He needed to find something.

"No. Impossible! Inconceivable," he would say, leaving me to wonder what his next argument would be.

Not only was he convinced that Douglas wasn't crazy, but he also avowed that my illness was summoned to enlighten me. And just so I didn't forget about this, he constantly reminded me of my fate.

I couldn't understand why Jean was so determined to convince me that I should do what Douglas had asked of me. No, I didn't understand why. But, whatever his reasons were, his impetuous arguments were beginning to work.

Only now, after all that has happened, when I look back in time, I understand why Jean was placed in my path. It wasn't just a coincidence that he became fascinated with my torments. He had been tormented himself, but didn't remember. Not yet.

Jean, the Chef, had been in the restaurant business since he was seventeen, he told me one day as I sat in his big kitchen appreciating his craft. His first job had been in a small café in Biarritz, a charming beach town in the Southwest of France, where Jean came from. At twenty-two, he moved up to Bordeaux to follow his passion and attend culinary school. His father, "the old man", as Jean called him, wasn't too thrilled about it, but finally agreed since this was the sixties, and chefs were becoming prestigious around France.

Jean talked about that time with nostalgia and I wondered how old he really was. I remember him telling me once, when

I made the mistake of asking him his age, that, he was as old as he looked and as young as he acted. "Young as I act, cherie." After that, he spun on his heel and waved the spoon in the air disregarding my question.

He also told me that he hadn't always been gay. At least, he didn't think so. He said that he had a girlfriend back in Biarritz, but that it didn't feel right. Then, he smiled, looked at me with sincere eyes, and told me that the day he woke up next to Ramón, on the Rue du Soleil, in the charming town of Bordeaux, he realized that that was it.

"I am gay!" He told himself.

The two of them—Jean and Ramón—were still together, and working on the cruise's cuisine. What a joy it was, to watch them in the galley, arguing over the proper way to debone veal, or glaze pork. It was fascinating. They kept the crew from boredom and they became my best entertainment as well as my really good friends. After their daily arguments were settled, and the commotion they caused in the kitchen had calmed down, we would gather on deck and marvel at the sky.

How wonderful it was! Being on the ocean—looking into the infinite, it was electrifying. There, in the middle of the sea, without any city lights, the stars were brighter and the darkness darker.

It was there, on the deck of the *Queen Leonor,* that I was introduced to French cigarette smoking, and it was absolutely impossible to watch how they consumed their cigarettes, without arguing with them. I tried to tell them that that much smoke wasn't good, but Ramón would look at me with pity and say: "Oh cherie! What is? What is?" and he would blow the smoke into the sky above us, and take another deep puff.

Ramón and Jean had been together since the night Jean discovered himself in Ramón's bed.

"It's been too long," Ramón would joke, making fun of their long time together. "I'm going to look for a new boyfriend," he teased Jean. "Brand spanking new!" and that would make Jean cuss in French, from what I could understand.

Their plan was to retire soon and move back to Jean's old town of Biarritz. They told me that they had a darling apartment facing La Grande Plage, Jean's favorite place on earth.

"You have to come visit us one day, cherie. You will love it there," they told me, and I promised them that one-day I would.

Work was hard. There were long hours and there was the annoying alarm clock next to my head reminding me constantly that it was time for another shift. There were the sporadic annoying passengers who really thought of themselves as royalty, there were Jean and Ramón's arguments in the kitchen, and there was Jean perturbing me about Magellan's secret, but still, I loved it! The cruise opened my eyes to a whole new world, a world I thought existed only in dreams. I decided, that I was a lucky girl. They could, after all, not have hired me, but no—I was among the lucky ones who had gotten a lucky ticket.

I felt safe on the ship. There, I looked into the horizon

and tried to figure out where my past ended and my future began—there, far away, where the sea meets the sky.

"One can only imagine what the navigators lived through," I remembered Douglas saying, back in my little kitchen. "Their desire, their uncertainty, their fear of not knowing where they were going or if there was even a place to go." And that's when I realized that I was safe only for the time being. The ship was my home only for that moment. I was living with the uncertainty and the dread of not knowing where I was going after my contract ended. I knew that I wasn't going to be there forever, but I didn't allow myself to think about it. *Not yet.*

Chapter 38

A River In Spain

SINCE THE CRUISE LEFT CÁDIZ, I had missed *Señor* Antúnez's family. I called them a few times, and I could not wait to see them again, and sit on their veranda above the sea. Soon the ship would return to their waters and I was counting the days. I managed to double up on a couple of shifts, and by the time we arrived at their port, I was free to get off the boat.

As soon as we arrived I called the house and in less than an hour Cristina and Agustín were parked by the dock, waiting for me. When I saw them, I felt a sense of comfort that I hadn't felt in a long time. I got in their car and left my temporary home floating behind me. As Agustín drove us through the streets of Cádiz on our way to the *Casa Blanca*, I realized how beautiful the place was and how hung-over I had felt the morning I left their house on my first visit. I vowed to myself to not let Cristina or Agustín serve me *claro* again.

The drive was taking longer than I thought and I asked Agustín where we were going, since I remembered the drive to his Grandpa's house being much shorter than the drive we were taking.

"It is a surprise," he said, as his foot pressed down on the gas pedal. "We will be there in no time, since I am in the driver's seat," he joked.

It was a bright summer day and the drive was beautiful. Everything was in focus. The wild daisies were blooming, making the day cheerful and the intricate architecture reminded me that the place had been inhabited by many different cultures. It was stunning. For Cristina and Agustín it was nothing new since they had grown up there, but to me, the place was exotic, vibrant and full of life. I couldn't tell where one place ended and another started as the villages all flowed into each other. Agustín wasn't the only one to be racing on the streets, every other car seemed to be in a hurry, but yet, everything was perfect.

Almost an hour had passed when I saw a sign that said, Sanlúcar de Barrameda. Vaguely, I remembered hearing or seeing that name before, but could not remember where or when. Soon after I saw the sign, our little white Peugeot came to a stop. In front of us there was a river flowing past, until it was swallowed by the Atlantic Ocean. Agustín got out of the car, lit a cigarette and opened the passenger door telling me to get out. I did it without hesitation since I was curious and it was getting hot inside the small car.

"See?" he asked me nodding his head towards the river's mouth. "This is it. Grandpa wanted me to bring you here," and he finished puffing on his cigarette.

I looked at the beautiful scenery in front of me and

wondered why the old man had wanted me to see it. I smiled slightly, not knowing what to say.

"Ok," I managed to say finally, as I watched the river flow.

"Grandpa just said that you needed to see this place, OK?" Cristina hesitated. Then I realized that neither she nor her cousin knew the reason why they had brought me there.

"Well. It is a nice place," I tried to be polite, which made both of them laugh causing Agustín to choke on his smoke. He cussed at the cigarette between his fingers, and said that he was going to stop.

"Tomorrow," he said. "Tomorrow I will stop," and he continued puffing on the thing.

"Ok then. Let's go!" Cristina said getting in the Peugeot. Less than five minutes had passed with us standing in front of the river, and then we were once again, stuffed into the little car driving back to Cádiz.

"It is funny that Grandpa asked me to bring you here," Agustín said from the driver's seat.

"Grandpa told me to not bring you home before you saw the river," Agustín told me, sounding puzzled himself. "Sometimes, I just don't know about that old man." and he shook his head, as if troubled that his Grandpa was perhaps getting a bit too old. I too wondered why *Señor* Antúnez had asked him to show me the place, but I stayed quiet not making much about it.

We arrived at the *Casa Blanca*, had not even parked, and Cristina was already out of the car.

"Come," she said. "Grandpa is waiting for us," and she grabbed my hand and rushed me up the narrow stairs, leading me to the veranda where their dog was resting under the large wooden table.

The bright magenta bougainvilleas, growing unconditionally on the trellises were still bringing life to the veranda and giving us much of the needed shade. The morning was bright and the sea in front of us was lit, revealing its secrets. The sound of the water touching the edge of town was becoming familiar to me. I heard it in my dreams and I heard it through my days.

Can I ever be apart from the sea again?

On the massive wooden table, there was a bowl filled with fruit, and on the barbecue, the charcoal was burning.

"There you are!" said *Señor* Antúnez, coming out of the living room. Behind him, I saw the painting, which had almost made me faint the night I had come to the house—the painting portraying Magellan's ship. Now, composed and delighted to be back in their home, I let the painting stay quiet on the wall, and didn't allow it to bother me.

Señor Antúnez walked to me and smashed my face with the kiss he gave me.

"Come, come." He said pulling me inside the house. "Come say hi to Isabel. She is in the kitchen."

We entered the kitchen and the moment *Señora* Isabel saw me, she cleaned her hands on her apron and gave me a big hug. She took me to the oven and showed me the dessert, which was baking. "Pecan pie," she said and smelled the aroma. "You will love it!" Then, she shooed us from her kitchen, telling us to go sit outside.

On the way to the veranda I passed it. There it was—the painting still hanging on their living room wall, begging me to look at it. I only allowed myself to take a glimpse through the corner of my eye, but I noticed that the gold engraved plaque on its frame was shinier than the first night I had seen it, but still I did not let it perturb me.

"Thank you for having me again, *Señor* Antúnez," I said honestly.

"Ah Marina, the pleasure is ours," he said making me feel at home.

"Tell us, how is work going?" he asked curiously.

"It's great," I said sitting on the comfortable seat facing the ocean. "But I can't believe it is almost over," I told him. "I have one more month of work, but I'm not sure I am ready to go back home yet."

"Well then," he said, "you can always stay here with us," and he got up and placed the sausages on the fire.

To this day, I think that if I had said yes, I would have been welcomed to stay at the *Casa Blanca*.

"Grandpa," called Agustín, from inside the house. "Why did you want us to take Marina to the river?" he asked puzzled.

"Well . . . She had to see it before she leaves," the old man said.

"But there is nothing to see," Agustín challenged.

"And I am sure she has seen better places by now," Cristina supposed, smiling at me.

"Marina," *Señor* Antúnez said, "that is the place from which Magellan left to conquer the world." He calmly finished placing the skewers on the barbecue and walked to the chair next to me and sat down, as if he didn't realize that he had just confirmed the entire path of my life.

It was just like that. Nothing else.

He poured us some *claro*, and despite my earlier vow, I took a sip of it.

My stomach was starting to roll again, but I got a hold of myself. I noticed that *Señor* Antúnez's eyes were facing the sea in front of us, but his mind was elsewhere—I wish I knew where. It was just like Douglas used to be when he faced the ocean. Their expression was wise, a wisdom I wished I owned. I had no words to say. I could not speak. I was trying to make sense of what had just happened, and why.

Gently, he touched my hand, bringing me back from my daze. He gestured, so I allowed my eyes to meet the place where his eyes had been. It was a far, far distant place.

"You know," he said, "there are things that cross our lives because we make them happen, Marina." He told me looking into my soul. "But there are things that come into our lives without explanation, but not without a reason."

I swallowed the dry air in my throat and *Señor* Antúnez continued, "Now, now that you have seen it, now that you know it is true, let it be Marina. Accept it. Don't be afraid to pursue what is there for you, for how boring life would be if we knew what tomorrow was bringing. Don't settle. Accept your destiny." He finished, and walked to the barbecue, where his dog had thrown himself on the cool tile floor waiting for a treat, and *Señor* Antúnez stroked his friend on the head.

How does he know? What is happening? Now that I have seen it?

Señor Antúnez took the meat off the barbecue and we lunched under the magenta flowers. As soon as *Señor* Antúnez finished his piece of pecan pie he left the house through the stairs, which led to the street. I watched him as he walked away, and I followed to the veranda's door and looked down the stairs watching him close the gate behind him.

"Where is he going?" I asked *Señora* Isabel, when I came back to the table.

"Oh honey, only God knows." She answered with a sad look in her eyes.

We sat there on the veranda looking at the sea, as the sun shone in our eyes hiding the sea's secrets from us. The wind had subsided and the water was becoming still, making the sound of the ocean quiet down—now, I only heard the water caressing the wall.

"You know," I attempted, "it is funny that your Grandpa wanted you to show me Sanlúcar—the place where Magellan left from." I said, not sure if I should bring it up, but they looked at me with expectation and so I continued.

"I have a friend back home who is fascinated with Magellan and Magellan's history. My friend swears on the grave of his mother that it is impossible that Magellan died without leaving any records of his voyage around the world." I swallowed and continued as their eyes were suddenly glued to me. "My friend says that at the time of the explorations, one of the most valuable things was a captain's log. My friend knows everything about the old explorers, but especially Magellan. He doesn't believe that Magellan's expedition around the world left no records, other than an account told by some Italian guy who survived the voyage." *I can't believe I am saying this.* "My friend Douglas insists that there is more to Magellan's last voyage. He believes that there must be some records, somewhere." I finished, worried about how they would react to my account.

"No way!" Agustín laughed, lighting a cigarette. "We thought only Grandpa was that crazy," he said, and gave a big puff on his cigarette, and continued. "Grandpa goes to the sea every single day! He tells us that he is going fishing, but somehow we keep eating sausages. He doesn't think that we know that he just sits there and stares at the ocean with his fellow fishermen. When we were kids, Grandpa told us the sea wanted to tell him a secret, and that's why he sits there. He is waiting to hear it again. Grandpa told us that the first time it happened he was just a kid—about ten years old. He said that he was chasing our grandma around the docks where they use to play, and he heard a whisper. He said that he looked around trying to figure out where the whisper had come from, but there was nobody. Nobody! Grandpa said that he kept looking around but he did not see anyone, and when he looked for grandma, she was gone. Grandpa says that there was an old ship anchored by the bay, which his mother had told him to not go near. Grandpa said that he went anyway. He said that he swam to it. When he got to the ship, there was an old man on it, and the old man waved him on board. Grandpa says that the old man's name was Jaime, and that he was the oldest person he had ever seen. He said that the old man told him stories of pirates and conquistadors, and stories of a lost land far beyond one's sight. Grandpa says that that's when he first heard the name Magellan. He said that the old man, Jaime, told him that Magellan had found a land that had been lost. The old man told Grandpa that one day he was going to find it. Grandpa says that the old man even showed him an old map with a drawing of the place on it. The old man told Grandpa that he was going to look for that land and that he was going to live there once he found it. They spent the whole afternoon sitting on the prow of the old man's ship, and Grandpa swears it was the best afternoon of his life. When Grandpa went home and told his mother, she was so mad that she spanked him hard and told him never, ever go by the old man or his boat again. Grandpa said that it didn't work, because the very next day, the first thing he did was to run to the dock, but when he got there the boat was gone. Grandpa said that he looked all over the bay for it but there was no sight of the ship or the old man. By the time he got back home, he had decided that he was going to be a sailor—just like the old man." Agustín said this without realizing the effect his words had had on me.

It was the second time I was hearing that Magellan knew about a lost land. Was everyone crazy? Was I crazy? Did Magellan really discover it?

"Grandpa says that when he told his mother that he was going to sea, his mother was glad the old Pirate had left because there was no way she was going to lose her boy to a crazy man like that. She had already lost Grandpa's father to the sea, and that's why she was so protective of Grandpa. He told us that his mom was so mad that she forbade him to go by the docks. Grandpa didn't mention the sea to his mom again," Agustín told me, while finishing his cigarette, which was now, almost burning his fingers.

"When Grandpa turned eighteen, he announced to his mother that he was going to sea," Agustín continued. "Then, she could not keep him any longer, and so he left. He told us that our great grandmother cried and cursed the old man, Jaime. He said that she was terrified to lose her child—since the sea had already taken her husband from her, but Grandpa went to the sea anyway. Luckily for us, as he puts it, 'Your grandma was so beautiful that I could not be away from her,' so every time he left Grandma, he counted the days to come back to shore again to be with her, and that's why Cristina and I, we are here today. So, his mom finally got what she wanted. He forgot about the sea, took over the family's market and married our grandmother, the most beautiful woman in Cádiz," and Agustín got up from his chair, and kissed his grandmother on her face.

I was stunned by the story. It was so involving, so revealing, especially because I was sitting there on his veranda facing his sea. I could imagine young Antúnez coming back home to his love.

"Grandma says that even though Grandpa left the sea, he never gave up on it because he goes and sits by it everyday.

When he comes home, he always confesses to her that he believed the old man, Jaime. Grandpa believes in the old man's stories, which he heard on the forbidden ship when he was only a boy. The old Pirate Jaime had his own theories about Magellan's voyage. Grandpa says that the old man told him that there is more to history than we know, and that, is what still carries Grandpa to the sea. The old man Jaime, and Grandpa, they have their conspiracies, their secrets." Agustín finished, leaving me dazed as I pondered Douglas' secrets and conspiracies.

Chapter 39

The Kingdom of Love

IT WAS TOO MUCH TO TAKE IN. Too much to swallow, but I did. I sat there on their veranda and listened to the stories they wove for me.

Why? Why am I hearing all this? I argued with myself.

The day was going by fast and I did not want to go back to the ship. I wanted to know more, I wanted to hear it from *Señor* Antúnez, but he didn't come back—he was sitting by the sea.

Señora Isabel, who had been listening to our conversation, told us that some nights, when she and *Señor* Antúnez were laying in bed, he mumbled just before drifting off to sleep, that the old man Jaime must have been right. That Jaime must have found the place, and that's why he never returned.

"Antúnez needs to know before he leaves this world that the old man wasn't crazy. If Antúnez dies without knowing, he will never rest," *Señora* Isabel said, with a sad look in her eyes—a look that begged for help. She wanted this for him—for the man she loved.

Cristina, who was sitting quietly listening to our conversation, jumped to her feet and out of the blue she told her grandma, "That's it Grandma! The old Pirate Jaime and Marina's crazy professor must be related," and just like that, she walked inside the house leaving us with our mouths wide open with surprise, just to come back soon with an old raggedy piece of paper with a drawing of an Island on it.

"See?" She asked me as she showed us the drawing. "This is what keeps Grandpa dreaming—a piece of paper with his drawing from when he was a kid. He said it looks just like the one Jaime showed him." And she walked back in the house with the paper in hands, leaving me stupefied. I ran after Cristina and asked her if I could see the drawing one more time. I stared at it for a few seconds and then walked back to the veranda. I was puzzled. I felt as if I had seen that drawing before.

We spent the rest of the day talking about Ayrton Senna and about the great Brazilian soccer player Pelé. They knew all about the accomplishments of the two sportsmen. I found out that the family never missed a World Cup, and never missed any Formula One race, since Senna started on his ascension to the top.

"The races are only worth watching because of him," Agustín said with confidence, then he got up and told Cristina and I to get ready because he was taking us to town.

I kissed *Señora* Isabel goodbye, and left *Casa Blanca* with Cristina and Agustín. It was almost time for me to start my shift and in less than three hours we would lift anchor and leave Cádiz.

Saying goodbye to the Cartagenas was not easy. With a knot in my throat, I kissed the cousins goodbye, and watched them drive away from me.

My feet felt heavy as I walked onto the ship. It did not feel right to leave *Casa Blanca* behind me. *God knows when I will see them again,* I thought as my heart compressed a bit more in my body.

As I found myself on the pool deck of the *Queen Leonor*, leaving the Port of Cádiz behind, I didn't know what was going to become of me, but the cool breeze on my face blew away any sad thoughts I had, because I would always remember the afternoon at the Cartagenas' veranda. I remembered every word and every movement *Señor* Antúnez said and did, but most of all, *Señora* Isabel's words, were still pleading in my ears. "He will not rest until he finds the truth. He must know that the old man wasn't crazy." And the look in her eyes—I had seen that look before, I just couldn't remember where.

As we left the shore of Cádiz, I told Jean the story that Agustín had told me about his grandfather. The whole thing! Jean's only comment was, "And my mother thought that only my uncle was crazy!"

Jean's sarcasm towards his uncle was understandable. The uncle never showed his face and when he died he managed to put a hole in Jean's parent's finances, since they had to bring the old ship back to France, where it sat, until the thing almost deteriorated. But still, I wished Jean had a little more compassion for *Señor* Antúnez and his story. But instead, he was simply Jean. He didn't show his heart.

With Cádiz behind I soon got back into the ship's rhythm, and the Cartagenas became a good memory of my time on the cruise.

Jean's obsession with Magellan dissipated since he and

Ramón had decided that this was going to be their last season on the cruise. They were finally going to retire and go back to Biarritz, where they had plans to live a long and healthy retirement.

Elisa, she decided that she was not going back home to Brazil and she chose to go visit a friend in Italy who was living with some relatives. She did say that she was going to find herself a hot Italian man and forget about the old boyfriend, even though, it was obvious, that she still liked him.

Me? I wasn't sure what I was going to do. I knew that I had a ticket back to Brazil and more than a couple of dollars in my wallet, which should last me for quite a while, but besides that, there was not much more.

Our last two weeks of work were bittersweet. Nobody wanted to leave the cruise and go back to his or her ordinary lives. Unfortunately it was in our contract that we had to leave in order to return, and so, Elisa, Jean, Ramón, Carla and I managed to squeeze in every free hour that we had together. We had become a family, though, a very dysfunctional family.

Jean and Ramón smoked incessantly, and their arguments had multiplied in the last week. They were nervous to start their new lives together. After all, they had talked and dreamed about it so much and now that it was finally close to happening, it was obviously causing them anxiety.

Elisa was terrified about packing all her belongings and going off to Italy on a new adventure, but she did. She managed to pack all her stuff and somehow she looked as if she was finally starting to forget the old boyfriend. Carla was the most composed of us all. She just sat there and didn't say much. She was already used to the comings and goings of a life on a ship and was planning on coming back for a fourth season.

Still, with all the ups and downs of our moods and all the uncertainty of our futures, we pulled ourselves together and enjoyed our last moments as a family.

Our final night onboard the *Queen Leonor* was full of joy. Somehow, we managed to lift our spirits and celebrate the time we had spent together. We knew that perhaps we would not see each other again, but we also knew that our friendships were everlasting. We drank, we cried and we made fun of each other's awkward moments onboard. If Jean was in a bad mood, we all knew about it. We all knew when Elisa had waited on some very snobby tourist because she'd throw a tantrum saying that she was leaving the ship at the next port. We knew about all the men who had tried to sweet talk Carla. And they all laughed about the endless times I spent listening to the tourists pour out their life stories to me, while getting hammered by the drinks I served them.

Jean was in such high spirits that I loved him even more. I was able to read him finally, and what I found was marvelous. Jean was always going to be a part of me. No matter where we went, no matter how far apart we were going to be; I knew that he was always going to be my friend. There were no secrets between us.

As the ship cut north through the cool Atlantic water taking us to the Port of Lisbon, we rested with peace on its deck looking into the darkness and dreaming about our futures.

Chapter 40

My First Time In Portugal, 1988

IT WAS EARLY MORNING when the ship entered the River Tejo in Lisbon. The river was calm and the sunlight striking the city was making it look as if the city was about to pop out of the hills, but as we were approaching Lisbon's shore, the sunlight on the buildings changed colors, making the architecture more real.

I was sad to leave the *Queen Leonor*, and saying goodbye to Jean was the hardest thing of all. He had become a good friend, someone I could count on, and he, unlike anyone else, understood my demons. Jean insisted that I go to Biarritz with him and Ramón, but I told him that I had things to do back in Brazil, but that wasn't true.

I have nothing to do. Why did I say such thing? Still, I didn't accept his invitation, but promised that one day I would visit him and Ramón.

Carla, my Portuguese friend, also invited me to her family's home in Portugal. Jean quickly responded looking at me with fierce eyes, "Don't you dare!"

At first, I said no, but after she argued that a couple of days in Portugal wouldn't kill me, and after Jean had actually agreed with her, I decided to accept her invitation.

"Don't be silly, you will love Portugal." Jean said when I told Carla that I should go home.

They finally convinced me to stay and I realized that it was probably my only opportunity to see the country where my ancestors had come from, as I wasn't sure if I would ever see it again.

If I had any doubt about staying, it all vanished when I met Carla's parents. They had been standing by the dock, anxiously waiting for our arrival.

Miss Antonia, Carla's mom, was a large woman. Her black hair, woven with gray, was short and curled up. She sported some very intricate gold earrings, which caused her curls to appear even more pronounced. She looked exactly as I had imagined the Portuguese countrywoman to be. Her skin was beautifully wrinkled by the sun and her hands were strong. She wore a black dress with a burgundy scarf wrapped around her shoulders and on her feet she carried flat comfortable black shoes.

Carla's father, Mr. Alberto, was shorter than his wife. His grey hair was covered by a Portuguese beret, and the patterned gray pullover, he wore over his long sleeved shirt, had probably been knitted by his wife. He was a man of very few words, and it seemed that the few words he said, were either to tease Carla, or to prove to Miss Antonia that he was always right. They were a funny couple, and it looked like they had been together forever.

"Are you rich now?" Mr. Alberto asked Carla, when he first saw her coming off the boat. "You better save your money, or you're going to work at the restaurant with us," he teased her, giving her a hug that took her off the ground. Miss Antonia kissed Carla's face and did not let go of her daughter until she had to, when we had to get in the car.

They lived in a small town, a half an hour away from Lisbon, called Sintra. As Mr. Alberto drove us through the city's suburbs, leaving the capital behind us, the warm sun touched my face through the car's window, and I fell asleep. Carla woke me just before we arrived at her home—just as I was starting to have my nightmare. I was glad to be awakened.

Her parents' home sat in the lower part of Sintra where they had lived since they got married. They owned a small restaurant across the street from their home where they served traditional Portuguese food and wine. The food was prepared by Carla's mother and aunt, and the wine came straight from a barrel, which sat by the restaurant's entry door.

It was there that Carla grew up. There, she learned to cook with her mother, and there she met the man of her dreams, but apparently, the guy had turned out to be a nightmare. Carla showed me my room, which was across from hers in the hallway. The room faced the street, and from the window, I could see the restaurant.

The establishment was quite fascinating. It looked as if time had decided to stop around there. People went in, sat down and stayed for what seemed like forever.

"Dad has all these friends, you see?" Carla said, when she saw me staring at the restaurant. "They all have a tab. They come to say hello and they don't leave until the sun goes down," she shook her head and walked across to her room.

By the third day in their house, I understood what Carla had meant about her father's customers. I noticed the same people coming by. They sat down in their respective chairs by the sidewalk, and did not attempt to leave until the sun set. They seemed undisturbed by the traffic, and the pedestrians passing by. "They just hang around, you see?" Carla reaffirmed.

Chapter 41

The Moment of Truth

ON SUNDAY, MY FOURTH DAY, I woke up with Carla entering my room, sitting by my feet on the bed.

"Ok," she said with an intriguing look on her face. "Today you are going to meet the rest of the family. Please don't be afraid," she begged me. "And please don't take anything that my cousin says seriously."

I sat up on the comfortable bed and promised her not to pay any attention to her cousin. I told her to relax because her family couldn't possibly be that bad. She looked at me hopelessly and said, "Wait until you meet them!"

I peeked outside my window to establish that the usual customers were sitting in their usual chairs outside the restaurant, but I was surprised to find no one there. It felt awkward—as if part of the scenery was missing.

I learned later, that on Sundays, the business was closed.

I changed into my clothes and entered the kitchen where Carla was on the phone talking to someone. When she saw me, she said goodbye and hung up.

"Let's go," she said, and dragged me out of the kitchen.

All I could do was follow her, since she was already out of the door, determined to go somewhere.

"Let Marina have breakfast first!" I heard Miss Antonia yelling from the kitchen as we exited the house.

"We will eat something in town," Carla yelled back.

We headed for the upper part of town, where Carla told me we were going to meet some friends. As I followed her stern steps I couldn't help but notice how beautiful Sintra was.

The trees, shading the way to the old upper part of town, were losing their leaves to the sidewalks, and the weather was just starting to become cool with a refreshing breeze stroking our faces. We walked past cafés, where I could smell the sweet aroma of baking pastries, and we were crossing the valley, which led us to the oldest part of Sintra, when Carla stopped by a natural fresh water spring.

"You make a wish before you drink it and your wish will come true," she told me, holding the water in her hands before drinking it.

The fresh water was making its way down the hill through river rocks and green moss. It was crystal clear but I was not sure if I wanted to drink it. I wasn't sure if I wanted to make a wish.

What do I want? I asked myself, looking at the suspicious fountain, while Carla dared me to drink from it.

"But you have to make a wish," she encouraged me.

I put my hands under the spout and collected the water.

I paused.

I made my wish.

The water was cool, and it tasted like no water I had ever drank before. I tasted the moss, the green, I tasted the iron and rocks, and the time it took for it to descend from the hill, making its way through the obstacles. It was invigorating.

We continued walking until we arrived at the old part of town. It was breathtaking. It was the most beautiful place I had ever seen. One of those places that I believed existed only in dreams. It took a minute or so for me to come back to reality and realize that I was in fact, living it.

"Carla," I managed to say, pausing again to take one more breath. "It is wonderful!"

"It is, isn't it?" she said blithely, as if she were talking about some ordinary thing, and kept walking in front of me, rushing somewhere.

I was still in awe when I was taken by surprise by a horse drawn, open carriage, strolling by. The horses pulling the carriage were majestic, and the handsome young man driving it smiled at us as he took his beasts through town.

Time needed to stop. There was no need to rush. Everything was so perfect. Everything was so unreal.

The cobblestone paths that had been beaten by millions before, surrounded by the lush vegetation where the romantic buildings sat with their small windows peaking at us, it all made me feel uneasy. It was too perfect. As if there was no need for me to see much more in my life.

And, above it all, sitting on the hilltop, Sintra's pink palace suited the place without pretention—like a jewel in its exact setting.

"Come," Carla said, pulling me back to reality. "You are

going to try the best pastry in town," and she walked inside a café, where she was greeted by her friends.

We sat down among her friends and she ordered us two espressos and two pillows.

"Did you say pillows?" I giggled, as the waitress walked away with the order.

"Wait until you try!" Carla answered.

The pastry was delicious. It was shaped like a pillow and had a dreamlike filling, which I can't explain. The coffee was strong—a perfect match for the sweet pastry.

Carla and her friends were excited to see each other. They had been friends since they were kids, and they talked with ease, laughing about their recent adventures.

After we finished our coffee and pastries, Carla and her friends took me through the old walkways above the café. There, they told me the history of the place. They told me how the Moors had made the land their own a thousand years ago, and that there they had built their fort, where some of its walls still stand to this day. Carla told me that Sintra was a kingdom, where kings and queens fought their demons and enjoyed their affairs. Carla told me that she could not live anywhere else. Sintra was her home.

We said goodbye to her friends and we walked back to her house, where I was surprised by the voices coming from inside. The moment we entered the front door Carla was assaulted by the many kisses of uncles and aunties. They were telling her how they had missed her and how skinny she looked when they paused as they saw me.

"*A Brasileira,*" one of the uncles said, making me blush.
"Leave her alone!" Carla said at once, but they did not listen
to her. They all started asking me questions at the same time.
Some were intelligible questions, but some I could not comprehend, making me realize that even though we spoke the
same language, there were many differences between us.

I was surrounded by people. Loud people, beautiful people,
lively people. They all spoke fast and although half of their
words were foreign to me, I realized how interested in my
culture they were, which helped keep me afloat. When I did
not understand a word, they would come up with something
I did understand. They made me feel at home. They loved
Brazilian music—just like my friends from Cádiz, and they
were addicted to Brazilian soap operas.

It was an amazing afternoon. We sat around the two
tables, which I helped put together under the grape vine in
their small backyard, and we talked for the rest of the day.
We ate, we danced, we drank wine, and I realized the reason
Carla was so grounded was because she was loved so much.
Again, I felt as if I was home, a home, which I didn't have.

They were sincere and unpretentious, but then, there was
the cousin.

Luis was as charming as he could be; with his leather
jacket and his leather boots, a cigarette in one hand and a
glass of wine in the other, he looked wild and striking. His
jet-black hair was slyly wavy and perfectly groomed. His face
sported a beard, which was a couple of days old, giving him
the wild look. He was absolutely sexy. Someone that people

want to look at, but know is too dangerous to touch.

At the end of the day I was worn out. Being around Carla's family consumed all my energy, especially her cousin Luis. He had charmed me all through the afternoon. When I finally found myself in my room, looking out the window to the quiet street and contemplating Carla's family, I realized that I missed the witches. I decided that I was going to call them in the morning.

By the time I woke up, Carla was already up and ready to leave the house. It was as if she was in a marathon. She wanted to see all her friends, and she wanted to do all the things she wasn't able to do on the ship. But what about me? I just wanted to pause and perhaps join the people sitting across the way at her parent's restaurant, and make that call to the witches.

"Today we are going to Cascais," she announced over breakfast, which smelled delicious.

Dona Antonia, who was by the sink, turned and faced her daughter, "Carla!" she said. "Give the girl a break!" and she looked at me hopelessly. She knew her daughter better than I did, and she knew that nobody was going to stop her.

"Carla," I asked hesitantly. "Would it be OK if I stayed here today? I want to go back to town, and maybe go visit the palace."

To my surprise, she smiled, and told me that it was alright.

"You don't mind going on your own?" She asked, but without letting me give her an answer, she said, "Wait a minute, Luis would love to take you there!"

Luis was her fierce-looking handsome cousin. *Oh God, no!* I thought. But it was too late because she was already calling him on the phone.

"No, please!" I pleaded her. "I will be fine on my own."

Carla agreed to leave me in Sintra. She did confess that she had seen the palace one too many times, and she was glad that I did not mind going on my own.

We left the house together, and walked to the bus stop by the valley, where she was going to take the bus to Cascais and I was going to go my own way.

Carla was dying to see her old boyfriend, and since he was working in Cascais, she was going for a visit.

"This is your last chance, sure you don't want to come?" Carla asked me one last time.

"Yes. I will be fine. Look at this place," I said, gesturing around me, happy that I was soon going to be on my own.

I wished her good luck with the boyfriend and said goodbye. The bus left and I walked away and found a phone booth from where I made a call to the witches. The phone rang and rang, but there was no answer. I hung up the phone and I started on my odyssey. If I had known what I was going to be feeling later that day, I most likely would have stayed inside my room at Carla's house staring out the window into the restaurant, but instead, I dove into the most fantastic and alluring day of my life—a day that set my path in stone.

As I walked by the water fountain, from which I had drunk the day before, I couldn't help but stop. Although there was a line of people waiting to make their wish, I had to drink from it again. I knew I was being silly, but I waited my turn anyway, and the girl in front of me started to tell me stories about the fountain. I let her explain her version, which was completely different from the one Carla had told me. The girl told me that the water coming out of the spout was royal water. She told me that if one drank enough of it, good fortune would come his or her way.

Ok then, I told myself. *Today I will drink a bit more than yesterday.*

I drank from it and continued on my discovery of Sintra. As I walked the road leading me to the majestic old part of town, life seemed still in front of me. The old women at their front doors dressed in black looked at me with quiet eyes.

The gardens all around me were old. Their autumn colors; they conveyed a magical but sinister look. I decided that such magnificence must have been planted generations before me. The buildings, with their red-fired roofs, were safely tucked within each garden, and it seemed as if inside each structure, there was a story waiting to be told. How many lives had passed through them? How many stories could they tell? Sintra made my blood flow faster and my heart beat stronger. I wished then, that I could share my feeling with the world. I was completely happy.

I walked to the taxi stop, and approached a cab whose driver was comfortably snoozing. I knocked on the window and the man was startled from his daze. I asked him if he could take me to the palace.

"Of course," he said, and immediately got out of the car

and opened the door for me. The car was an older yellow Mercedes Benz, with seats made of leather.

"Nice car," I told him.

"German built." The man replied proudly.

The road to the top of the hill where the palace sat was covered in leaves. Old green leaves, yellow leaves, orange and brown. I wanted to ask the driver to stop so I could go and play in it, but I restrained myself. The street was mostly shaded by enormous trees, which contributed to the magical, yet sinister atmosphere of Sintra.

I kept absorbing everything around me as the car ascended to the top of the kingdom, and I had lost myself in a fairytale world when the taxi came to a stop and the driver told me that we had arrived. I paid the fee, got out of the comfortable car and felt the cool breeze around me.

The surrounding vegetation seemed untouched. It was as if someone had come from above and dropped the palace in the middle of it. It was absolutely stunning. As I crossed the draw-bridge, I was dazed by the grandeur, the beauty and splendor of it, and it was there, beneath a lurid, yet protective gargoyle, that I felt again a bit closer to Douglas.

It became real to me, that once upon a time, there was a kingdom, and that once upon a time people had surren-dered their lives to it, just as Douglas had surrendered his life to what he believed was true. There I learned that perhaps he wasn't as crazy as I thought, since the surroundings bared love, passion, and desire. There I realized that passion comes from within and desire is what develops from it. Douglas's passion became clear to me up on that hill, and his desire to conquer his passion had pulled me to him like a magnet.

From there, through the mists, I could see the old town submitting itself to the kingdom. It was there that I finally surrendered myself to my destiny. Douglas understood me, and he read my need for a navigator. He knew I had desire and that I just needed to find my passion.

I forgot time and the day flew by without giving me any hints of its passing. It was late in the afternoon when I exited the palace and found no one around. I decided to start descending the road to town, and was hoping someone would pass by and give me a ride. I had been walking for a while and was wondering if I would make it to the village before night fell, when a taxi came driving up the road and stopped by me. Inside, the same driver who had driven me to the palace earlier in the day was raising his eyebrow at me.

"I didn't see you coming down to town, so I thought I'd better check on you." The man said with a concerned look. I smiled at him and got in the back seat and we drove down to town. By the time we arrived at Carla's house it was already dark. I had started to pay him for the ride when he smiled and said, "Go on *Brasileira*, the ride is on me." I thanked him and walked to the front gate of Carla's house.

"Where have you been?" Carla asked, with a worried look on her face. "I was wondering if I should send the guards to look for you!"

"I am sorry, I didn't realize it was so late," I told her honestly. "The palace! The palace is beautiful!"

She shook her head in disbelief and I thought it was better not to talk about it. What could I tell her? That I had fallen in love with the place? That my days in Sintra were numbered and I didn't know if I was going to be able to leave it?

"Listen," Carla said, "we have no time for dinner." And she rushed to her bedroom and I followed her. "Get ready, we are going out. Luis will be here soon." She announced.

I did not ask her where we were going, because after ditching her in the morning, and being gone all day, I thought it was better to listen to her.

Luis came through the front door like a hurricane and the scent of his masculine cologne travelled throughout the house without redemption. He looked even more handsome than the day before, but also more dangerous and more insatiable.

We left the house and I was commanded to sit next to Luis in his Mini. As we left Sintra on its wavy road it felt as if the little vehicle was going to tip over with every curve Luis made. He was racing against himself, since most of the drive was clear of other cars. I prayed that we would get to wherever we were going alive and quickly, because there was absolutely no hope of him slowing down.

Thankfully we made it to our destination without any major happenings and I was pleased to finally free myself from Luis's maniacal driving and his petite car. We walked on the streets of the Bairro Alto, and we hopped from bar to bar until Luis found his friends. Carla's ex was one of them, and she was delighted that he took hold of her as soon as we walked in, and cuddled up to her all through the night.

When the night was almost over, or so I thought, we walked to the little Mini again, and I made the sign of the cross before getting in. I wasn't looking forward to the drive back to Sintra, but Luis promised not to race back home. Well, there we were again—at every turn, I tried to distract myself from Luis's fanatical driving, and even Carla—who was used to her cousin's driving ability—was scolding him, pleading with him to slow down. There was no hope.

I finally relaxed and then came to realize that Luis actually drove well, despite the small size of the car and the impression that it was going to tip over at every turn. I found him to be extremely charming. He wanted to please me, and he was doing it without effort.

As we started for the Coastal Highway, Luis abruptly turned the Mini toward what I was convinced was the wrong way. He announced that he was taking the "*Brasileira*", me, to see the monument dedicated to the Portuguese navigators.

Instantly I felt my stomach turn upside down, and I wasn't sure what had caused such havoc inside me, if it was the sharp illegal turn, which Luis had just accomplished, or the announcement he had made.

Why in the world does he think I need to see the monument? My heart was playing with me, and it seemed then, that the whole world was complying with Douglas.

I don't want to see any fucking monument!
I don't want to know about any fucking navigators.

And suddenly my mind started to speak in a kinder tone.

I just want to go back to Sintra. To a safe bed, to a safe dream, and tomorrow, wake up and go on with my simple life.

But no, there was no chance, for I was in really deep trouble. It seemed that someone was throwing the dice for me, and no, I was not happy. I was really scared.

It was late night, and it was as if we were the only ones awake. Luis drove the car on the sidewalk and parked right next to the massive structure. Now, I was sure we were going to get in trouble—if not for the wrong turn, then for the illegal parking job.

I got out of the car and I stared at the monument. It was breathtaking. Carved in stone, the figures of the men who had conquered the sea were facing the waters of the River Tejo.

It is real.

It was then that I realized that Carla was calling me from above the memorial. They had started to climb the colossal stones, which depicted their heroes and they were calling me to join them. Hesitantly, I climbed, feeling uneasy. Luis was the fastest one, and by the time I was halfway through fighting my way to the top, he was already contemplating the dark and calm water below.

It was a daring thing to do but when I finally arrived at the top, where Luis was, I caught my breath and sat next to him. It was amazing. There I was, where "everything started," as Luis had said. Among the navigators!

"This is not the end," Luis said, "this is where it all began," and he showed me the river in front of us. "And he, who went away to never return—the one our king believed was incapable, he showed the world, the freedom and the knowledge which men still pursue today, for he was the greatest, and he will be remembered forever." These words that came from Luis's lips sounded like a melody. He spoke them from the heart, and I wondered if those were his or someone else's words.

"May I ask who he is?" I said teasing him for sounding so romantic.

"Our Great Uncle, Magellan," Luis said, and I felt as if I had been struck.

Chapter 42

Reality

I WASN'T LIVING A DREAM. Douglas was real, Rafael was real, Cristina's grandfather was real and so were the stories that the old man Jaime had told him. Until that moment, it was all a little fuzzy—quite strange. But it all became clear. I could no longer doubt it. Everything made sense. Everything was leading me there. I had to live, believe and hunt for the truth. All the pain, the fights, and the uncertainty, it all vanished. I felt strong. I had a reason to be.

"Go get it," Lucien's words were whispering in my ears again.

"It is your turn to steal it," Douglas words daring me, pleading me.

"You will cross the seas," the beautiful gypsy lady said to me while the money slipped from my fingers.

"Uncle is crazy!" Rafael's words not sounding too convincing.

"Now that you have seen it, now that you know it is true, let it be Marina, accept it. Don't be afraid to pursue what is there for you, for how boring life would be if we knew how it would be tomorrow. No, not good. Not good."—*Señor* Antúnez's words finally making sense.

"They had challenged their wisdom, they were the greatest of the explorers, but Magellan was the one who connected it all," Douglas's words sealing my resolution.

Douglas, Douglas is right. I will look for him when I get back. I will do what he wants me to do.

As we drove back to Sintra, fine and lazy dew was kissing the entire town. It was even more magical now, since everything became clear. Less than a year ago, it all had been scattered on my kitchen table, back at the beach of Canasvieiras as Douglas so passionately taught me what was there for me. It was there, walking with the fish in my hand, that I saw Douglas again, and the course of my life was set. There the Fortune Teller revealed my destiny. Now, I felt entitled, now I needed to know the truth.

As I kissed Luis good night at the steps of Carla's home, his words were replaying in my ears like music. "My great uncle Magellan," he had said.

Gently, he touched my face pushing away a strand of hair between us.

I liked him. He was original and not afraid of who he was. We kissed again and I walked inside the house knowing that he too was going to become my past. There was no time for feelings. There wasn't time for play.

As I rested in bed that night, and the events connecting me to Douglas's madness ran trough my mind, I felt foolish for having let them torment me. There was no return. No looking back.

A couple of days later, as Luis parked in front of Carla's

house to take me away to the airport; I was consumed by a strange emotion. As I stepped down the front steps of the house leading me to the gate where he was standing, I felt as if I was descending a mountain where the air had been thin. I knew what I was doing and what I was going to do. I knew that the chase was going to be dangerous, but I had to go on.

I left the house and did not look back. I knew that Carla and her parents where watching me from their window, and I didn't want to miss them more than what I was already missing.

Luis held my hand and told me not to leave.

"You can move in with me," he said modestly, showing me his sweet side, which I knew he had.

No. I wasn't going to stay.

I'm leaving now, and only God knows if I will ever come back.

Chapter 43

She Doesn't Know, Does She?

AM I GOING CRAZY? I asked myself again and again. *Have I walked these same steps before?*

In front of me, Roland was walking with the same entitlement he had shown in the airport in Casablanca. I should have run away, I should have screamed for help. I should have, but I didn't. There was no more fear in me.

Entering the house, where I had the feeling I had been before, I saw my life vanishing because of my stupidity. My life, my dreams and possibly even the secret would die with me. *How could I have done this to us? Now Douglas will never be free, I have worked so hard to get it, and what is Roland going to do with it?*

I walked through the narrow archway that led us to the back of the building, where Roland told me to wait.

I have to run. I thought. But I didn't.

"We just don't say no to Land," his grandma's words, rang in my ears as I stood waiting—just as he had told me to do.

Roland returned bringing a woman. She was dressed in black, and she looked harmless, but what did I know?

He ordered me to follow her, and again, I did as I was told. The woman did not say a word, but my demons; they were talking up a storm. "No, you are not going to die," they tormented me.

I didn't realize that Roland was following us until I sat down as directed, on the wooden chair inside the small kitchen. He was right there, standing behind me—overpowering me. The room was small and with Roland in it, the place seemed even smaller—claustrophobic!

The woman in black poured me a glass of water, which I did not touch, then, finally, she looked at Roland and spoke.

"Poor thing! She looks so tired," she said shaking her head. She continued talking but I could not understand what she was saying—I was too shocked by my inaction. She faced the window in front of the sink as if searching for someone outside of the house. She turned back from the window, looked into Roland's eyes and asked him, "She doesn't know, does she?"

He looked at me and said, "No. Not yet."

He walked to the fridge and poured himself some water.

"We will wait until he gets home. He is on his way," he said, and left the kitchen.

Nothing was making sense. I wished there was some sort of feeling that I could grab on to, to save myself, but there was nothing. It felt as if my soul had simply detached from my body and had not even bothered to let me know where it had gone. All senses had vanished when I opened my burgundy carry-on in the back of João's atelier and realized that Magellan's letter was gone.

It had been such a long journey to find it. Six years! Six years searching for the truth. Six years of my life wasted in the submission to his dream. *And now I don't even think I am going to die!*

Chapter 44

An Empty Trinidad, 1988

AFTER LEAVING THE *QUEEN LEONOR* and spending the wonderful time in Portugal with Carla and her family, I returned to Brazil. As soon as I landed in Rio de Janeiro I took a taxi to the Marina da Glória where I went looking for the *Trinidad*.

"Miss, do you want me to wait?" the taxi driver asked as I stepped out of his cab.

I looked around for the *Trinidad*, but the vessel was not to be seen.

Rafael must have taken it out for a ride, I thought.

"No Sir, thank you," I said, and paid the driver.

I stood by the empty dock with my luggage by my side. The taxi driver gave me one last look but I waved him off, barely containing my excitement. I couldn't wait to see Rafael, and tell him all about my trip and all I had discovered.

It had been almost seven months since I had last seen him, when he said goodbye to me as I boarded the *Queen Leonor* to Europe. I was eager to tell him everything—to tell him about the people I had met, the places I had been and to tell him that I believed in his uncle Douglas. I wanted to tell him that his uncle wasn't crazy, so I sat on the dock and waited.

There was hardly anyone around, and the boats anchored by the docks looked like they had been abandoned. As I sat there I wondered if Rafael was going to be happy to see me. After all, I had not told him that I was coming.

The sun was getting low in the sky and the jet lag was starting to weigh on me when I finally saw the *Trinidad* entering the harbor. The boat was a monument. No wonder Rafael loved it so much. She was like a queen walking down a street, while everyone lined the way and bowed. Majestic, with it's sails down, wading through the calm water—coming home.

I pictured Rafael standing on the bridge, shirtless and with his contagious smile on his face.

"You're crazy, *chica*, I can't believe my uncle did this to you," he would say, after I told him that I was in, that I believed in his uncle and that I was going to help Douglas pursue his dream.

As the *Trinidad* touched the dock, I had a moment of unease—I felt foolish for being there waiting. Still, I could not leave, for any moment Rafael would appear, and would greet me, and all would be OK. But on board the *Trinidad*, I only saw strangers. A couple of people stood around the deck and someone else threw the large rope to tie the boat—not Rafael.

"Hi," I said when the stranger leaped on to the pier next to me.

"Hello," he returned with a smile as he rolled the thick cord around the post.

"Can you please tell Rafael that Marina is here," I asked him feeling awkward because I was hoping to see Rafael doing the job.

"Ah Miss, Rafael doesn't work on the *Trinidad* anymore," he said, inspecting me with the edge of his eye.

"He went sailing up North with his uncle a couple of months ago," the man said finishing the job, and leaving me speechless.

My heart squeezed in my chest. I felt a knot in my throat, threatening to suffocate me. *How foolish I had been to think that he would be here, waiting for me.*

I was hungry and exhausted. Desolation was weighing me down and all I wanted to do was to go home, but I had no home to go to.

I walked to the pay phone and called a cab. In less than a few minutes I saw the yellow car driving into the harbor and the driver took me to a small inn nearby. I entered the lobby and started to pay for a room but then decided that I didn't want to spend the night in Rio. There was nothing else for me there.

That same evening I returned to the airport and bought a one-way ticket going south. South was the opposite direction of the man I was searching for, but I did it anyway. I went back to Florianópolis—to my beginning with Douglas.

Chapter 45

Back on the Island of Florianópolis

I GOT A ROOM IN A SMALL HOTEL in town and slept for two days waking up only to eat and use the bathroom. On the third day I decided that it was time to start living again. I got out of bed, opened the curtain to let the light in and felt lifeless standing on my feet, but a long hot shower helped to lift my spirit. I changed into some clean clothes and went down to the lobby. I asked for directions to the closest restaurant, and walked to the old restaurant-bar nearby that offered fried fish as their special. I smiled remembering Douglas telling me that too much fish was not good for me.

I was starving. The food made me feel as if I had returned home. I ate, and after, walked out to a pay phone where I called the witches. They were happy to know that I was back in Brazil, and to me, it was comforting to hear familiar voices. I promised that I would call again soon, and that I would go visit them, but they knew I wasn't ready to face that place yet.

I had to decide what to do with my life, but all I wanted was to see Douglas again. Unfortunately he was sailing north and God only knew if he was ever coming back again. I was troubled, heart broken and lost, but a small thread of hope took me back to Canasvieiras, where I thought that if I had any chance to see Douglas again, it would be there.

"You're back!" shouted the fishermen when they saw me walking in the local tavern. Suddenly I felt illuminated, as if the mist, which had been obscuring my mind, had lifted itself. The bright smiles on their tanned and lined faces told me that they had indeed missed me. Dona Marta, the tavern's owner, heard the commotion and came from the kitchen. She rushed over as she saw me, and enveloped me in her comfortable warm embrace.

"Dinner is on the house," she announced to the patrons. "Come," she said reaching for my hand and leading me to the kitchen, where she showed me the empty gas tank—which served as a seat in her precarious, but functional kitchen.

"We missed you girl," she told me. "The beach has not been the same, since you and Douglas left."

She had to say his name! She had to bring him up!

"Oh girl, you can't leave us anymore," she said turning the fish in the frying pan. "I hope you came back to stay," she told me, but I didn't know what to say, so I left her without an answer.

"So, tell me, how was your job?" she asked making me happy to remember my time on the cruise.

I told her about my days in the ship, the people I met and I told her about all the places I had been, as I took small bites of the fish on my plate.

"Miss Marta . . . " I hesitated. "When did Douglas leave?" I finally asked her.

"Oh, girl, that crazy man? He left right after you left to work. Maybe a month after?" she said, with a pleased look in her eyes and continued. "He ate here on his last night in town, and said that he was going up north to pay a visit to some nephew of his. He was acting kind of strange—even for him," Miss Marta told me. "The men said, that after you left, he never helped bring in the net again, and that he just sat there, on the sand, with his eyes fixed on the ocean."

I swallowed the moist air in her kitchen and tried my best not to show her how uneasy her words made me, but my mind was killing me with thoughts of Douglas, sitting on the sand—by himself.

"I knew he was crazy the first time he walked through these doors," Dona Marta said with conviction. I nodded my head as if I agreed with her, since I knew that that would make her happy.

Miss Marta's words started to fade away, as I lost myself remembering Douglas.

"Do you know how to clean it?" he asked as he walked next to me looking at the fish I held by its tail.

"You have much to live for," he told me as his hands paused on the old map.

He had taught me all he knew—all he could.

"Give him a call if you're around," Douglas told me at the airport, giving me the piece of paper, with João's address on it.

But I never did. I never called Douglas's friend in Portugal.

I had been too busy walking and dreaming on the streets of Sintra and left Portugal without paying João a visit.

Miss Marta brought me back from my daydream and we walked to the front of the restaurant where the fishermen were happily asking me all about my trip. I told them all I could as their eyes envisioned a far, distant, untouchable world, and when I was leaving Miss Marta's tavern that night, her husband Mr. Afonso said, "Come early one morning, help us drop the net, Miss Marina." His son, who had been playing billiards by himself, shook his head in disagreement.

"Dad!" He shouted. "You know women cannot come on the boat. They bring bad luck."

"That's no woman son!"

"Afonso!" shouted Miss Marta.

With the knife she was using to cut limes waving in the air, she said indignantly, "Don't you dare talk to the girl like that!"

"It is OK, Miss Marta," and I smiled at Mr. Afonso, forgiving him. I kissed them all good night and said that I would try to show up early one morning. Carlos looked at me as if saying "Don't you dare!" and I walked away leaving him to his billiard game and his superstitious mind. Instead of going back to my apartment, I went for a walk on the beach. The smell of the ocean, the sand hugging my feet, it was all comforting, but still, I felt ungrounded, and I had to figure out what my next step would be. I needed to find Douglas.

Chapter 46

Witch Power

How INNOCENT I WAS. Douglas wasn't coming back.

I got a job on a local cruise schooner in town, where tourists from all over the country came to experience the beauty and hospitality of the Southerners. It was a great job, and I thanked my stars for finding it so easily, since unemployment in Brazil was at its height and most people were barely surviving.

The schooner sailed at sunset, taking people for a special evening on the waters around the island. It was a stable job, the pay was good and it kept my feet on water. I made new friends and enjoyed my days on land before venturing back to the sea. I went to the beach and walked the streets of the island in search of nothing. I tried to keep myself busy and I started to enjoy life again as my hope to see Douglas was slowly dissipating.

Foolish me! Knowing what I already knew about my life, I should have been more suspicious. Life had never been that simple. I was caught up in my own lie.

The day my witch called me moved slowly. I walked to the beach, ate a sandwich at the luncheonette before going to work, and after the day was done, I went home to sleep. I had just dozed off when the phone rang.

"Hello," I answered half asleep, and was startled by her voice. It was Carmen, my favorite witch and the youngest of all the seven witches. She was calling to say that we needed to talk.

She was the one who came to visit me before I left for my interview with the cruise line in Rio de Janeiro. The one who told Douglas that I was strong as any man, the night Douglas told her that I was going to do big things, and the one who brought the curse of the witches upon the sisters. She was the seventh consecutive woman to be born from the same mother.

"I will be there by noon," she said, making me worry about what was so important that she could not have told me over the phone.

We said goodnight and I lay in bed restless trying to figure out what she wanted to talk to me about. I fell asleep and woke up late.

When I entered the bus station, Carmen was already waiting for me with a dazzling smile on her face and her porcelain skin glowing. She looked happy, which confused me, for all night I had been thinking that there was probably some kind of trouble she wanted to share with me.

Carmen told me all the news of her sisters and herself, about her and her sisters' recent life endeavors, which was not much, and then she shared all the gossip from my old town with me. She told me that the people who had moved into my pastel colored house were very annoying. She told me about how the city had finally stopped talking about the tragic event of my life and that I should perhaps come back to town where I could possibly feel safe once again.

"No," I told her. *Never!* I thought.

She smiled and touched my face, inspecting my features and patted me on my back telling me that it was all right. I finally relaxed, for until then I had been expecting bad news. I looked at her and searched for any signs that would explain why they were called witches, but found none, other than the wise look she carried in her eyes.

To this day, I am not sure if she and her sisters were witches or not. If they were, they were quiet about it. They kept their lives to themselves, their mysterious home closed, and they drew their curtains at the sight of curious eyes. Yet, they managed to intimidate the town's people.

When they walked to the marketplace they had an air about them that made most people move out of their way. Everywhere they went they seemed to leave a mystery behind them. Yet, they did nothing out of the ordinary.

There was not much that people knew about them, other than the fact that their mother had died when Carmen was born, and that their father had gone mad shortly after. They were left on their own to care for each other, and without any family or friends they closed themselves within their walls and accepted the speculation of neighbors without any care. It was almost as if they were from another time and place, not allowing people's ignorance to bother them.

Just to complicate things, they were beautiful. Even the eldest of them carried her head high and her posture straight. Their patrician bodies were covered by much of the clothes they wore, and their hair, which they kept long, was controlled in a tight bun above their necks. Often it seemed as if they knew more than everybody else, just like they knew to bring the laundry in before a sudden storm or to open the door before the mailman knocked on it.

Carmen hugged me and told me that she missed my curious eyes searching for them as I strolled in front of their house before I'd gone to live with them. I told her that I missed them, too.

I asked her about Arcelio, her one platonic love, and she made a face at me.

"Of course I knew about him!" I told her. "I saw how he used to look at you when you walked by the bay," I revealed making her happy.

Poor Carmen! Being cursed, no man was ever going to be brave enough to approach her. All they had the courage to do was to watch her as she strolled by their boats. Her black silky hair, her white porcelain skin, her beautiful long and lean body—covered by her garments, caused men much pain, but she was a witch. Arcelio wasn't brave enough.

"We have a gift for you." She told me, and put an envelope in my hands.

"My sisters and I, we will never have children," she told me with sad eyes. "You are our only trust. You need to find the truth and we want to help you. We want you to follow your purpose. You cannot stay here. You must go. You have to do what you were predestined for," and she kissed me goodbye leaving me on the platform speechless with the envelope in my hands.

"I know you will be wise." I heard her saying as she vanished into the crowd. I held the envelope in my hands, and watched her silhouette disappearing.

I went home and left the envelope on my table for a week, but eventually I opened it. With the money the witches had given me I went back to Portugal. If I was going to become a thief, I needed to know that the letters really existed. I knew that searching for them was as close as I was going to get to Douglas.

I had finally become aware of how much I was capable of, how little I had to lose, and how deep into Douglas' soft sand I had sunk. Magellan's letters, which Douglas had recited, had become part of my being. It was as if I was right there with Magellan, following every curve of his pen as he wrote down his words to his beloved ones, confiding his secret. I had become the ink, and the tip was tattooing my path. I was going to follow his dream, but still, I wished I knew why.

Chapter 47

The Search, 1990

It was early morning when I landed in Lisbon, my second time in Portugal. As I walked out of the Lisbon International Airport terminal the bright early morning was sharp and clear and I knew what I was there to do. I felt energized and empowered. I grabbed a taxi to Estoril, and the driver took me to a charming bed and breakfast.

The Inn was a two-story home that sat on the hills above the Estoril. The driver politely carried my luggage and walked in front of me to the lobby. I paused at the entrance capturing the surroundings. The old white mansion, shaded by the lush trees and the tall splendid palms sat surrounded by the intricate ironwork of the fence. Iron chairs sat scattered around the gardens as if begging to give someone the time to sit and marvel at the serenity and romance of the place. They were intentionally placed there giving anyone a chance to slow down and to dream.

I walked in and was greeted by a teenager with too much eyeliner. She wrote down my name on a piece of paper and gave me a key to the room telling me that it was on the second floor, then, went right back to turning the pages of the fashion magazine that was keeping her busy.

Just like this? I thought. No identity? No information?

I climbed the wooden stairs and found room twenty-two. It was large and dark. I searched for the light switch and turned it on, noticing the high ceiling with the brass chandelier. The wood floors squeaked as I walked in. I tossed my bag in the corner by the dresser, took off my boots and dropped my jeans on the floor. I lay under the blankets and the last thing I remember was gazing at the ornate chandelier.

When I woke up, someone was knocking on my door, and for a minute or so I couldn't remember where I was. Slowly my mind came back to me and even more slowly I put my jeans back on and opened the door. I found a concerned lady standing in front of me asking me if I was OK.

"Yes. Thank you. Just tired," I said, still dazed from sleep.

"Come," she said. "Come eat something." and the woman walked away, making the old floor squeak.

I closed the door and lay back down on the bed again for a few minutes—surprised at my being there.

What am I doing?

Then I remembered.

I got up again and left the second floor and room twenty-two to go search for the lady who had woken me up. I found the kitchen, where the girl who still had on too much eyeliner, was sitting by the table arguing with the lady. The woman, without any hesitation, gave me a welcoming smile, ignoring the teenager, and showed me a chair by the table.

"Here, I hope you like it," she said, and placed a plate of food in front of me.

Ah, it smelled delicious! Codfish and potatoes—a true Portuguese specialty. I ate two servings and remembered the first time I had codfish at Carla's parents' restaurant, and before I could finish it, the lady placed a piece of pie in front of me and started to tell me all about how she ended up in that kitchen in that Inn.

The attractive hotel, which she was so proud of, was inherited from her husband's parents. It was there that her husband grew up, and since they had inherited it, they decided to turn the charming home into a hotel. It had been a dream they had and the location was perfect for the business.

"People love to play at the Casino," she told me pleased. "It keeps us busy."

The Casino do Estoril was just minutes away. She told me that people from all turnings of the world showed up at its doors, bringing them business, all year round.

"And you?" she asked me nosily. "What brings you here?"

The question grabbed me by surprise.

What am I doing here?

"Not sure yet," I told her, making her face tense—showing the worry lines on her forehead.

"Well," I tried to calm her. "I am here to help a friend trace some documents for his job." I lied.

I can't believe I just lied to the nice lady!

What could I tell her? That I was going to be looking for something I wasn't sure even existed?

No. I could not.

So I lied.

I didn't realize then that it was an expertise that I would be developing. It was all lies.

The night was cool and I was still tired from the trip. I finished my dinner and thanked Miss Otilia for the hospitality and I went back to room twenty-two where I collapsed back to sleep. I don't remember dreaming that night.

When I woke up the next morning I opened the wood shutters and was astonished by the view. There, in front of me, the sea glittered and the morning was brilliant—welcoming me.

From the hill where the Inn sat I had a view of the magnificent coast. To my right was the beautiful town of Cascais, delineating the edge of the coast. A few boats were anchored by the shore, and outside—in the middle of the blue sea a few lazy sailboats were waiting for the breeze to pick up.

It was absolutely alluring. I braced myself on the windowsill and stood there for a while, then, I started to hear noises in the hallway and remembered that breakfast would end soon. I dressed quickly—clean jeans and a white shirt—and went downstairs to the kitchen.

Miss Otilia greeted me as she prepared my breakfast and I asked her directions to the Museu da Marinha. It was at the museum that I was going to start my search for the letters. I finished my breakfast and walked to the station where I took the train to the museum.

When I got there, the intimidating building that housed the Maritime Museum was disloyal to me. I found myself lost among the old displayed vessels without knowing what to do.

It was nothing like I imagined it would be. I thought that I was going to get there and magically find all the information I needed regarding Ferdinand Magellan's life. Perhaps, even his logs would magically appear—after all, it was around there that Douglas had spent much of his time when he was in Portugal working on his master's degree. What a fool I was.

I did enjoy wandering among the elaborate boats and their history, but I felt betrayed. I decided that I was wasting my time and that I needed to make a plan and make it fast.

I left the building and walked across the gardens to the Padrão dos Descobrimentos—the monument, where Luis had sang the life of his "Great Uncle Magellan," the night we climbed to its heights. Now, in the daylight, I could clearly see the portrait of the navigators who had faced the mysteries of the sea.

I walked around it and sat by the edge of the water where I tried to plan my search. If there was something in Portugal that would lead me to confirm Douglas' hypothesis, I needed to find it. I realized that I could not do it by myself. I decided that I needed to find Douglas' friend, João. I looked through my black address book and found João's address in it, written on the piece of paper Douglas had given me the day I left Brazil to work on the cruise.

I jumped on the train to Cais do Sodré, and from there I walked all the way to the address I had in my hands. When I arrived I noticed that although the door was closed, it said "open" on it. I peeked through the old etched glass and couldn't see anyone inside. Hesitantly, I slowly opened the door and a jangly noise resonated. A gentleman came walking briskly to the front of the store where I stood; not sure if I should be there, and he asked if I needed any help.

"Hi," I said to the man. "I am looking for João," and I hoped that he would tell me that there was no João around, hoped he would tell me that I should just leave, that there was nothing for me in Portugal. I wanted to disappear. I was making a fool of myself.

"Marina?" he surprised me.

"Yes," I answered cautiously.

"Douglas told me about you. Come. Come in," and he pulled me into his store, motioning that I should walk in front of him through the back of his stuffy shop, to a small hidden courtyard. He told me to sit and fetched us coffees from the café next-door that he shared the cozy courtyard with.

"Douglas told me about you. How is the job on the cruise?" He asked me.

I told him that it was great, but that my contract had already finished and that I had already gone back to Brazil.

"Ah, I see . . . " he said to me. "So what brought you back?"

I looked at him and timidly told him that I was looking for something.

"A new job?" he asked me.

"Not really," I answered, and I looked around as if for protection.

Could I still pull myself away?

What could I tell him? That I thought his friend was mad.

That I hated his friend for having trusted me with his illusion? That I was there to try to redeem myself for not having stolen the letter then, when Douglas asked me to? That I had turned mad myself?

No. I could not, so I stayed silent.

We drank our coffee while João told me stories about his and Douglas' youthful audacity. He made me laugh, telling me about how Douglas always managed to get what he wanted and that even though he thought Douglas was crazy with his wild ideas, he'd go along and somehow he was always the beneficiary.

"You see? The man has this thing about him that makes people want to be near him. It was easy for us to travel because we could always sleep in someone's house." João smiled, remembering. Finally someone was introducing Douglas to me.

"Yes, he does." I agreed.

"I miss him," João said, "but he is too stuck on this thing, this project, and he says that he has no time to visit."

"He misses you too," I told him.

I knew that Douglas missed him even though he hadn't mentioned it. I saw it in his eyes the day he gave me João's address and told me to visit him.

I finished my coffee, stood up, and said goodbye to João. It was a nice visit and I was content for not mentioning the real reason why I had come to see him.

João walked me back through his shop and kissed my cheek goodbye, telling me that if I needed anything, not to hesitate to come by.

"Thank you." I said, and was walking out of the store when I stopped by the glass door.

"I forgot to tell you," I said turning back to face João. "Douglas said that you are going to be the first one to know when he puts his hands on it," and I gave him a sad smile, and turned to go on my way when he stopped me.

"Oh no, he didn't!"

João took my arm and searching for an answer on my face he gave me a look of sorrow, knowing that Douglas had dragged me into his world. "That bastard!" he shouted.

I felt strange—without words to speak. I stood there waiting for João to tell me what to do.

He took my hand and pulled me back into the store. He closed the door behind us and turned the sign to the side that read "closed" on it. He showed me to an old rocking chair next to piles of leather and he sat down on a wooden bench behind his counter.

"What has he told you?" he asked.

"I guess he told me everything," I said, lowering my eyes, fixing them on a beautiful crafted Portuguese tile work with the words "*Casa do Carmo*" painted on it.

"Idiot!" João cursed, bringing my eyes back to him. "He still insists on it, doesn't he?" and he paused as if realizing something. "I thought that it was only his excuse to not come back to Portugal."

João walked to the back of the shop where he grabbed a wooden box. He brought it back and put it on the counter in front of us. The lid was covered in leather. He opened it cautiously and took a pile of yellowed postcards from inside it and started to show them to me. There were so many of them. João had sent them to himself knowing that one day they would be all that was left of his and Douglas's adventures around the Old World. There were postcards from Spain, France, and England. Postcards from Holland, Italy, Greece and Morocco, and there was one postcard from Sagres—one he hadn't sent himself. Douglas had sent it to him from his sailing trip with the Medeiros. On the back, Douglas told João that, "I just scored gold, and I will tell you all about when I get back."

"When he got back you should have seen him. There was this strange enigma surrounding the man. He told me about what Mr. Manuel had trusted him with, and he told me that he was going to find it. Since then, Douglas has changed. It is almost as if he breathes it in order to live." João sighed. "I told him that he was being a fool to believe in Mr. Manuel, but he wouldn't listen to me, so I had no other choice but to help him. We searched all over town for any evidence that could prove that Magellan had found this lost land he was talking about, but there was nothing. Nothing other than Mr. Medeiro's words, but Douglas still looked for it, even after he went back to Argentina. One day he called me and told me that he had finally found one of the letters Mr. Manuel had spoken of. It's been eight years, and I still remember him telling me how he almost had it, but was caught, having to leave it behind. When he called me last year telling me about you, he didn't mention it, so I thought that he had finally forgotten about the whole thing." João finished.

"Yes, I know it." I confirmed.

He looked at me, and I saw at the corners of his smile a little sarcasm tempting his lips.

"Yes, I guess he did tell you everything." João said.

"He also asked me to help him," I said, startling him. The smile vanished.

"He is out of his goddamn mind!" João said, and then looked at the ceiling of his shop for God's forgiveness.

"How old are you? Twenty? Twenty-two?" He asked me, but didn't give me the chance to answer.

"Don't you dare go getting yourself in trouble!" he scolded me throwing the postcards back in the box and slamming shut its lid.

"But . . . " I muttered, "I am starting to think that there could be something . . . " I shocked João with my confession. "If it is true what Douglas told me, why are the letters locked and lost?" I challenged, making him sit back on his stool and look at me suspiciously. "Imagine if Douglas is right," I continued, "It would give peace to him, and it would give peace to . . . " I stopped short as I was taken back to the veranda in Cádiz, where *Señora* Isabel told me about *Señor* Antúnez's ghost; the old man Jaime, who had disappeared out of the map—never coming back to tell *Señor* Antúnez if he had found the land or not.

"Yes. But is it worth running the risk?" João was asking me. "Is it really worth it?"

I didn't know if it was worth all that was being asked of me, but I needed something to be attached to—something to keep me going.

"If it helps to make you forget it," João said, "after Douglas left, someone called me from the Portuguese archives, where we had been looking for anything that would support Mr. Manuel's words. The person told me that there actually was something missing from the archives, a letter or something like that. They told me that they had a copy of the document and if I wanted, I could look at it."

"Did you see it?" I asked him anxiously.

"Yes," and he looked at the picture of him with Douglas, which was tucked in the wall among his leather goods.

"Here," he said, and opened his box again and took out an old folded paper from inside it. "I was able to make a copy of it."

My hands were shaking, my temples were throbbing, and my heart started to race.

I took the paper from João's hand and stared at it.

It looked to be a letter from Magellan to his friend Serrão, telling him the reason why he was taking so long on the South coast of the new continent. It was one of the letters Douglas had told me about.

I stared at the piece of paper in my hand and deciphered the old, almost illegible words on it and somehow it looked familiar. Could it be that I was so deep into Douglas's madness that I believed I had seen the letter before? I turned it over hoping to find the map Douglas believed existed on the back, but it was blank.

"You didn't copy the back?" I asked him shocked feeling my hands trembling holding the paper.

All the evidence that there was in the letter was at the end. I read the letter again and was stunned by Magellan's last words. There, all I needed.

"You must have sent a copy to Douglas," I told him.

"No." João said coldly.

I stood in front of him questioning the authenticity of his answer.

"Why not?"

"Because I told him that there was no map." João sighed. "I read it to him, but he didn't believe that the letter would simply fall into my hands." João shook his head indignantly and I saw his lips tensing on his face. "He argued why would the archives have called me and offered a copy of the letter. He said that it was probably bogus, so I never sent it to him."

"But you saved it!" I told him. "You saved it because you believed that it was important," I dared him. "You believe that Magellan may have found the land, but you are afraid of revealing it, aren't you?" I told him with disbelief that I had just called him out regarding his courage.

"Take it," he said. "It has done me no good." And he put the letter in an envelope, sealed it and gave it to me.

Without a word, I put the envelope in my bag and left the

leather shop. My heart was still racing in my chest, but this time it was excitement. I couldn't wait to show it to Douglas.

So much easier than I thought it would be.

I took the train back to Estoril and walked proudly up the hill to my beautiful Inn.

Now. Now I was going to find him, give the letter to him, and tell him that I was in.

Chapter 48

One Last Time

I HAD THE COPY OF THE LETTER Magellan had sent to his friend Serrão in my hands, and no matter what, I was going to find Douglas.

I had stopped again in the Marina da Glória harbor when I landed in Rio de Janeiro, but the *Trinidad* wasn't there, and there was still no sight of Rafael. I was hoping that he had returned from his trip up North with Douglas and that he could tell me where to find his uncle, but I was told that the *True North* had not returned and there had been no sightings of Rafael or his uncle. I left the harbor unsure if I was ever going to see them again.

I went back to Florianópolis hoping that perhaps they may have skipped Rio de Janeiro and gone straight South. I went back to Miss Marta's Tavern, and asked her if Douglas had come back, but the answer was no. I went down to the harbor where the men had repaired his boat the previous year and asked them if they had seen him, but, no, the answer was no again. A feeling of hopelessness started to take over me, but I kept on moving knowing that one day I would find him.

I had changed, and so had my vision of the entire scenario.

There was no more doubt lingering over me. I knew Douglas was right, and I knew that one day I would find the truth.

More than one year had passed since I last saw him, the day I left to Rio to work on the Royal cruise line on board the *Queen Leonor*, and God I missed him. I missed him unconditionally. I wanted to show him the photocopy of the letter that João gave me. I wanted to tell him that I wanted to know more. I needed him to convince me to go back and steal the letter for him, but I simply couldn't find him, and so I sat on the white sand beach where I had watched the canoe coming from the horizon and lived my life day by day, longing to know the truth.

The white sand beach was still the same, but still, I saw it differently. The sunsets were golden, just like before—surrounded by the rainbow of colors on it. But somehow it was as if I was seeing all that in black and white, just like a negative film waiting to be developed, and one day, it did.

Maybe he is back in Argentina? I asked myself, looking for an answer in the distant horizon.

I rushed back to my little apartment where I had returned to live, and stared at the envelope where João had put the photocopy of the letter Magellan had sent to his friend Serrão. The envelope sat on the same table where Douglas' old maps and books had occupied during my lessons. There, right on the envelope was Douglas' address. João had indeed addressed it to Douglas but never mailed it. I read Douglas' address over and over and came to the conclusion that I couldn't wait any longer. I was going to Argentina to look for him.

I was going to find him whatever it took.

I bought an old Alfa Romeo, packed it up and decided that I was going to drive to Argentina. I decided that if I didn't find him I was going to forget about him and start a new life, but first I needed to pay a visit to my witches. It was going to be my first time back to where the angels sang above the church's bell, and where I had killed the son of a bitch. It made me uneasy, but it had to be done.

I drove into the town over the worn cobblestone but I couldn't face my childhood yet, so I made a little detour and drove by the shore. I saw that the fishermen were still sitting aboard their vessels, working on their nets while waiting for the tide to moisten their boats again. Then I passed the church, resting quietly by the shore, still protected by the angels. By the time I stopped in front the yellow pastel colored home where I had once been happy, I finally broke down. I knew that my witches were safe inside their home and I knew that they were watching me. I took a deep breath, inspecting the pastel house for one last time, knowing that I wouldn't find what I was looking for and let it fade away.

It was time to forget. Mom was gone, the house was gone and the Marina that had lived there was gone. I got out of the car, straightened myself up and knocked at the forbidding front door of the witches' home.

The door opened slowly—only wide enough for me to enter. I walked into the living room where I had awakened the morning after I killed the fucking thief and my body started to shake. I didn't realize that I was still wearing the bleached blonde wig I had bought to protect myself from my old town. I took it off and I saw my witches' faces brighten, welcoming me. The place was still cold and pewter, but I felt safe in their house.

They hugged me and they were happy to see me, but they knew that I wasn't going to be there for long.

We sat in their dining room and I told them everything— just as I had told Jean, the Chef, after I woke up from my illness on the cruise ship. I told them all that I had gone through since I left town and I told them everything about Douglas.

Not surprisingly, they simply sat there and listened to my stories, and after I had finished, Carmen said, "Yes Marina, we knew about him. We knew that you were being reeled into a world bigger than the one we lived in. We knew you were going to do big things just like your mother used to say, and just like Douglas said the night I visited you on the Island." Carmen told me, and her elder sister continued, "Go. Go look for him." She said with her wise eyes approvingly.

They had known all the time.

Had they foreseen it?

As I drove past Lucien's house on my way out of town, I saw Lucien playing in the yard of his white brick beach house with the beautiful family he had grown into, and again I remembered his words: "When you want something you have to go get it."

As his eyes followed the Alfa Romeo, I faced the road and didn't look behind. I was going to get what I wanted.

Chapter 49

Back In the Kitchen Where I Did Not Die, 1991

MY LIFE! I THOUGHT, as I searched for an answer to why Roland had stolen the letter from me, and why he was going to kill me. With his every demand, I had simply obeyed him, hoping that he would tell me what to do. I wanted someone to tell me what to do, someone to take care of me. *But him?*

"Please, upgrade Miss Marina's ticket," I remembered his words at the airline counter in Casablanca, Morocco. He was so confident, so certain that I would not argue.

And his grandmother Mary? She looked so caring, so darling. She too had deceived me.

I couldn't understand why I had been so vulnerable, so fragile. I realized that there was nothing I could do, so I kept still, staring at the refrigerator door without knowing that my strength was going to be tested again very soon, and that the hunt was just starting.

All that I had gone through so far was just the beginning; just the teasing test.

Roland walked out of the kitchen, leaving me alone with this lady that I still thought could not be bad.

"Water, tea, coffee? Would you like something to eat?" she asked me with a concerned tone in her voice.

Who is she? I asked myself. *No. I don't want anything to eat. I just want to disappear.*

Still, she kept treating me as if she cared, as if she was really concerned about my well being—making me feel confused.

I could not grasp what was going on and obviously didn't expect what came next.

In the other room, I heard Roland opening the front door and welcoming someone in. There was silence, and I felt my skin beginning to tighten, as the instinct to fight was starting to prevail. Suddenly, I awoke to the realization that I was still alive, and I couldn't simply let myself die.

I continued to hear indistinct voices coming through the cement wall. The people in the next room were speaking softly, and I tried unsuccessfully to discern what was going on. Next to me, the lady dressed in black relaxed. "The waiting is over," she said.

"He is home," she said, and left me alone in the kitchen while she walked into the next room. I heard her tell the men that I wasn't looking well.

"Why didn't you tell her?" She asked someone and I heard Roland's voice reply.

"I thought it was better to wait for him."

"That bastard!" said a male voice, which sounded familiar.

My skin now was cold, and my sight was becoming blurry.

Sitting on the chair, still looking at the refrigerator door, I couldn't understand what was happening.

Stupid me. I had not thought of the aftermath. All I had focused on was to steal the letter, and now that it had fallen into Roland's hands, I realized that all I wanted it for was to keep me moving. Keep me going.

Who is Roland? Who is this lady who keeps calling me "poor thing"? And whom are they talking to?

I am no fucking poor thing!

I stood up from the chair and walked slowly to the door and quietly peered into the next room where Roland was talking to a man with his back to me. As Roland saw me gazing at them he stopped. The man turned and I saw his face. It was Douglas' friend, João.

My heart shattered. I thought there were no more places for scars, but I was wrong. The realization that I had been betrayed, lied to, and used, gave me strength.

I did not die in the closet, back in my old town. I am not going to die in this fucking kitchen. That, I knew.

I turned away from them and with the last light of the day vanishing outside the kitchen door, I realized that the door had been open the whole time. I was not in a prison.

The voices in the other room had stopped, but as I turned my back on them, they started to whisper again. I took one step in the direction of the kitchen door, and then another. Slowly, I walked out onto the porch and I saw that a small gate at the back of the yard was open to the alley. Steadily, I walked toward it, not making any sound and not hesitating.

As I passed the small gate I found myself running for my

life. I ran as fast as I could and only stopped when I could no longer keep going.

Night had fallen, and in the ancient, empty street where I found myself I saw a light shining at the end, where I found a phone booth. I fell into it with barely any breath left and closed the glass door behind me oblivious to the fact that I would not be protected inside it.

I had nothing with me other than my carry-on, since I had left my luggage at João's atelier earlier in the day when I had rushed out of his door.

I opened my small, black leather address book, and attempted to call Luis.

Come on Luis pick up. I prayed.

After an eternity I heard, "Hello?" on the other side of the line. My rushed breathing slowed down immediately.

"Luis, hi, this is Marina," I said. "I . . . I need help."

"Marina!" He exclaimed. "Where are you?"

"I . . . I'm in Óbidos."

"You are back!" he shouted and I could hear the excitement in his voice.

"Yes, I am here," I cut him short, still gasping for air. "Luis, I need help. Can you come get me?" Tears ran down my face but he didn't see them.

"Sure," he said.

I walked to the entry gate of town and waited in the dark. The tears had stopped running down my face, and a feeling of hate started to fight inside my being. I sat next to the massive stone wall which protected the city of Óbidos, and tried to figure out why Roland and João had betrayed me. What was so important in that letter, that the friend, which Douglas believed he had in João, had betrayed him.

When I saw Luis parking next to me my heart lightened up. I ducked in the car, and Luis started to Sintra. I wished then that he could drive even faster. There was not a long enough distance between Roland and I.

Luis helped me out of Portugal. I didn't tell him the real reason why I was back in his country. Again, he asked me to stay, and again I said no.

Now, more than ever, I wanted to flee. Run away, run away and hide. João had fooled me. Roland had fooled me, and I wasn't strong enough to face them and their truths.

Chapter 50

Argentina

THE LADY GREETED ME by the door and invited me in. She was beautiful, and she reminded me of Douglas—an earthly Douglas. Tall, slender, with shoulder length brown hair, and a smile that was soothing.

"He said you would be coming," she told me, as she closed the door behind us.

I gave her an uncertain smile not knowing what to say and followed her into the living room. Everything in it reminded me of Douglas, from the old maps framed on the wooden walls, to the nautical brass décor, to the old dark wood floors throughout the room. But it wasn't on water, and that's why he left.

"I am sorry to be troubling you," I told her, "but you were my only hope in finding Douglas," I confess her.

She put a small smile on her lips and her eyes travelled to a distant past—a past where she and Douglas had been happy, and a past where Douglas was still a part of her life.

"Yes he said you would come," she repeated. "He said that you were the one who trusted him." She told me. I smiled, understanding her skepticism toward her husband's ideas, but stayed quiet.

"Here," she said, and walked to the foyer, where she opened a drawer and brought back an envelope. "He left you this."

I looked at the envelope and saw my name written on it. It was Douglas' almost-illegible writing. I opened the envelope and my heart started to pace.

Marina,

I know that you made the most of your time on that cruise, and that by now you understand that the world is a bit bigger than you had imagined. I miss you dearly and I will take with me all the evenings I watched you devour my lessons; all the evenings you made me feel alive. You wanted to learn so much. You were my perfect pupil. I know you will do that favor for me, I will learn if it is true through you. Things will fall into place. Don't be afraid, be brave, my darling. I know you will know what to do, and then you will rest too.

Love, Douglas

I lifted my eyes from the letter and looked at her. A tear dropped from her eye.

"He is gone Marina." She finally broke.

*   *   *

Douglas had gotten sick; years ago when he was still a professor at the University of Buenos Aires. After learning that perhaps his life could be cut short, he could no longer live without pursuing what was destined for him. His marriage had been quiet and steady, but it wasn't enough. He was water and she was earth. Their daughter also didn't understand his love for the sea, and left him without giving him a chance to show her the magical world that could be hers. In me, he found the perfect Pupil.

Douglas and his wife kept in touch through the few letters Douglas wrote her, and the few phone calls he placed. When Rafael brought him home to Argentina where the long love of his life took care of him until he died, Douglas told her about me, and now, she was standing in front of me—accepting me.

She told me that Rafael had the *True North*, and that he was sailing around the world.

"He has taken over his uncle's dream," she told me, and she invited me to stay for supper.

That evening, she shared stories of her life with him—him, the man who made me into the person I am today.

I started back to Florianópolis the next morning fighting tears all the way, but when I found myself in front of the little beach apartment where Douglas had told me all about the world, I broke down. I walked in the house, which I had moved back into, and wept.

The next morning I crossed the green grass field where I had seen the gypsy family sitting under the tree. It was there that the Fortune Teller had told me my fortune. I was finally on my way to the Monastery. I was going to steal the letter Magellan had sent to his wife.

Chapter 51

Aftermath. April, 1991

THE WORLD SEEMED DIFFERENT to me. But no, I was the one who had changed. Waking up at the Copacabana hotel room after stealing the letter somehow left me feeling as if there was a hole in my chest. I spent the day in the room and only left when it was time for my flight back to Portugal.

As the taxi driver drove me through the crowded lively streets of Rio de Janeiro I felt lonely. I felt detached from the reality that surrounded me, and now, Rio de Janeiro was like a different city—not so illuminated, for I knew that Jesus now was crying on top of the Corcovado, looking at me through his sorrowful eyes. Now, I wasn't only an assassin, but also a thief.

What had become of me? Where did the innocent girl running up and down the dirt road go?

The knot in my throat was suffocating me, but it no longer bothered me since I had become used to it, and my tears for Douglas had stopped. Now, with the letter in my carry-on, I was on my way to Joãos' shop. João was the only person who could help me and perhaps tell me what to do with it. Now that I had finally had it, I could care less if the world would stop rotating.

"I have it João! You are not going to believe it." I told him with excitement when I called him that morning. I was still thrilled about it. I was proud for a moment, but now not so sure anymore.

The driver dropped me by the terminal and I slowly walked to the airline counter, conscious that at any moment I could be caught. I was, after all, carrying something I had stolen. I walked to the gate and sat down in the crowded waiting area. The terminal was busy, and people around me looked happy to be on their way to somewhere, but I wasn't sure if I was going the right way.

Alone, waiting for my flight, sitting in the air-conditioned airport, I felt hot. The chills I had had in the morning were starting to kick in again and as I tightly held my carry-on on my lap waiting for my flight, I prayed for God's forgiveness.

As the flight started to board I hurried to the line, forgetting about God. The grip on my carry-on was starting to burn my hand, but I only eased on it when the plane took off from the runway.

When I landed in Casablanca, Morocco, the last stop on my way to Lisbon, I rushed to the bathroom feeling nauseous. A man offered me a few inches of toilet paper by the ladies' room, but I ignored him rushing in the door and splashing cool water on my face. I had not slept for hours, and I was starting to feel exhausted.

As I left the bathroom, the man standing by the door wished me a "nice trip" and I stopped for just a moment placing my carry-on next to me on the ground for me to dry my hands, and that's when Roland snatched it from me.

Chapter 52

Two Letters

As I said in the beginning, Roland knows everything about me. He knows how much Douglas meant and how much I suffered after learning that he had died, leaving me to the mission to free his soul from hell.

Roland knows what I went through to steal the letter he had taken from me and he doesn't give a damn about it.

But what he doesn't know is that this is the last time he will see me, how much I hate him and that I finally found the letter Magellan sent to his friend Serrão.

It took me years but I finally remembered where I had seen it.

The letter was framed in an old wooden frame in the room I stayed in on the *Trinidad*, years ago, when I went for my interview with The Royal Cruise Line. The letter was framed with the map facing out, and that's why it took so long for me to remember that I had seen that same drawing before—the drawing of the lost land.

It all came to me when I woke up one night after having an anxiety attack. Through the hot and cold chills, my racing heart and the hopeless feeling, all I could picture was the map. I knew I had seen it.

I finally realized that the drawing Cristina and Agustín's Grandpa had copied from his Old Pirate friend Jaime, was exactly the same drawing that caught my eyes when I was leaving the *Trinidad's* room where I stayed. I remembered stopping and admiring it just before leaving for my interview with The Royal Cruise Line.

The drawing was stuck to the wall of the *Trinidad* and it pictured the same island, the same piece of land that young Antúnez had copied the afternoon he spent on Jean's crazy uncle's haunted ship.

It was the land Magellan believed existed further South of Patagonia; the land that the crazy Pirate Jaime wanted to find. Jaime had stolen the letter from the Portuguese archives, leaving only a copy of it. This copy did not have the map on its back, and that's the copy that the archives sent to Douglas' friend João. It was one of the letters Douglas had devoted his life to and thanks to my madness I realized that the drawings were all the same.

I have to get the map!

It had been years since I last went to the Marina da Glória harbor in Rio de Janeiro, and I was thankful to see the *Trinidad* resting at the dock when I arrived. Onboard, I found Paulo, the skipper who had replaced Rafael. He told me that Rafael had passed by the year before with the *True North*, the sailboat he inherited from his uncle Douglas—and that Rafael had left Brazil to go sailing around the world. Paulo was kind enough to invite me onboard, and I asked if I could visit the cabin that I had stayed in before in my stay with Rafael.

"Sure," he said smiling. "Make yourself at home."

I entered the cabin and there it was, still affixed to the wall. I looked around and Paulo was still busy on the deck so I carefully unscrewed the frame from the luxurious honey wood wall, and gently took the backing off the framing, allowing myself to at last see Magellan's true words.

Brother Serrão,

My bones are aching and my skin is drying on me. The men are becoming aroused, for the delaying is weakening their soul. I must though, not depart from here, where I am close to the lost land, which I believe I will find. The days are arduous, the sea is brave and the ships are screaming, but I must my friend, I must see the land where riches are buried. The land, which my Queen had told me about—the land where everyone was free. Look my brother, look at the map, for this is where I sit, waiting for the storms to pass so I can further in. Pray for me my friend, your brother of so many wars, your brother of so many misfortunes. Believe me, and you will be the one to come conquer the land with me.

Yours,

Fernão

My heart was beating slowly—it had finally learned to control itself—but I had not. My skin was hot, and yet I shivered.

Reading the letter and looking again at the map, which Magellan had drawn, I understood why Jean was placed on my path, and why he became so fascinated about Douglas's theory. The old Pirate Jaime and Jean's crazy uncle were the same person, and it was on his boat, the *Trinidad*, that young Antúnez had spent hours listening to the Pirate's stories.

I placed the letter with the map in my purse, walked unashamed onto the deck and thanked my helpful new friend for allowing me to visit the *Trinidad*.

"You are welcome!" he said as he escorted me out of the caravel.

As I walked out of the *Trinidad*, I left behind me the spirit of the old man Jaime sitting on its prow, looking at me with a content smile on his raggedy face. Then I called Roland and told him that I wanted my letter back.

I had finally gained the strength. It was far superior to the strength I had when I ran away from the kitchen in Óbidos, where I told myself I wasn't going to die.

Roland wasn't going to stop me anymore, and to my surprise he didn't argue with my request.

Chapter 53

Amsterdam, 1994

──────────────── Back in the beginning ──────

I PUT THE ENVELOPE IN MY PURSE and finished drinking my beer. I got up and turned my back on him. I knew he watched me leave. Only then he realized it was the last time that he was going to see me.

I was finally free. Free from him and free from the fear I felt about revealing the truth. It was the beginning of a new life. A life without ghosts, a life without anxieties. As I stepped outside the pub, the cool breeze felt exhilarating—but somehow with all the freedom there was an emptiness growing inside me. The emptiness of the end of a mission. The emptiness of not having any more perspective, or any clarity, of what to do next.

Years had passed since I saw Douglas for the first time, and years had passed since I learned about the travels of a man who connected us all—Magellan. In my hands lay the truth for what I had been searching. As I sat on the bed in the cozy hotel room in Amsterdam, looking out the window hoping for an answer why I was led to where I was, I held the envelope in my hands afraid to finally end the path that I had traveled for years of my life. It was the first time I was going to allow myself to read Magellan's letter to his wife, since I had been too afraid to even look at it the day I stole it from the monastery. It remained in the safety of my burgundy carry-on.

Hesitantly I opened the envelope and found two letters. One letter had been written centuries ago, but the other was recent. It was a letter from Roland to me.

I chose to read Roland's letter first, and as I read his words, they softened my soul and closed the gap that I had felt since I met Douglas.

I put the letters gently down on the bed; afraid to damage them, and stared out the window again.

I was finally free, I had read Magellan's words to his wife; the same words Douglas had recited to me back in my little kitchen years ago, and I finally started to understand Roland.

I placed the letters back in the envelope and back in my bag. I walked to the window, and stood there facing the street where the soft drizzle was covering town.

Then, before I knew what I was doing I was running out of the room and back to the pub, but the seat where Roland had sat earlier, where he watched me walk away from him, was empty.

I needed to find Roland.

I got back to the hotel room where I sat awake for most of the night evaluating what my life had become. I thought about the people I had lost and the people I wanted back, and the next morning I left the room and hopped on a flight to Lisbon. I was going to find him.

Chapter 54
Roland's Letter

I HAVE NEVER BEEN SO SURE about what I wanted in life as when I stood in front of Roland's grandmother's apartment, ringing the bell, but yet, I still felt strange. I stood with my heart in my hands and waited for the door to open. Slowly I saw Miss Mena appear from behind the door and she looked much more frail than the first time I had met her. She looked at me and asked, "What took you so long?"

I had no answer to give her. I had no answer for myself.

I walked inside the apartment and was embraced by the same warmth I felt on the first time I came in with Roland.

"Honey!" Mary said rushing to me. She hugged me and kissed my cheek, as if she had been waiting for me to arrive. "You look so tired," she said, holding my hand and bringing me to the living room, to the flowery sofa where Roland had sat comfortably years ago.

"How have you been, dear?"

"I've been OK," I lied to her.

"I have asked Land about you, and he told me that you have been too busy," she told me.

"A little," I said, again lying. "Is Roland home, Miss Mary?" I finally asked her.

"Oh honey, he left for work yesterday. He won't be back for a couple of months," she revealed. "You know how it is," she said. "They will close the station, and he won't be able to come home until the end of the winter," she continued. "It worries me that there are no flights in or out," she sighed. "I should be used to it already, but I don't think I will ever be," she said not making any sense.

What is she talking about? Which station? Until the end of the winter?

"What do you mean Miss Mary?" I asked her cautiously.

"Oh, honey, you know . . . at his work. They all stay there for months," again she wasn't making any sense.

"No, I don't know, Miss Mary," and she realized then, that her grandson hadn't told me. She realized then what a stranger her grandson was to me. Miss Mary looked at me puzzled and I wished I knew what went on in her mind.

"Of course!" she said shaking her head. She finally realized I had no idea what she was talking about.

"Come Marina, sit down."

I followed her and sat on the inviting flowery sofa, which was so empty. I sat facing her and she started.

"Marina, Roland has gone to Antarctica. He's been working there for years now. He is contracted by the Antarctica U.S. research station where he is a drilling engineer, honey," she revealed to me. "He won't be coming home for months. The weather gets pretty bad down there, and soon there will be no more flights in or out." she told me and reached for my hands. "He left yesterday morning for Amsterdam. He told me that he was having a very important meeting. He was acting a little strange, distant. He told me that the meeting was probably going to change his life," she paused. "Oh honey, what has he done to you?" she said when she realized how lost I was in her words.

"When . . . when is he coming back?"

"Oh, who knows honey?" she said looking at a picture of Roland sitting on the side table.

"How long are you staying?" she asked me walking to the entrance where I had left my luggage and she reached for it.

"Oh, no Miss Mary, I wouldn't . . . "

"No honey. Not the Ritz again. You need to rest."

I followed her to the guestroom and I noticed that the room looked the same. Miss Mary left the room understanding that I needed some time to myself and closed the door behind her. I sat on the bed and opened my purse where I had put the envelope with the letters. I took Roland's letter out of the envelope and read it again.

Marina,

It has never been my intention to hurt you. When I first saw you at the airport in Casablanca, I wasn't sure if you needed me. From João's description of you, I pictured a much more fragile woman, but there you were—strong, eloquent and autonomous. I reached for your carry-on because there was no other way to get your attention. I felt like a fool inviting you for coffee and was confused by your acceptance. As you laid your head on my shoulder on the flight to Lisbon, I never felt so tense, and holding your hand in mine I realized that I was the one who needed to be cared for, not you. But it was Douglas's wish. He knew that you were going to pursue it, and he wanted to make sure you were safe once you did it. Douglas knew that he wasn't going to be in this life much longer and he knew that once you had the letter in your hands João would be your only contact. Douglas wrote a letter to João confessing how he regretted pulling you into his madness, but he knew that it was too late by then because you were already reeled in. When you called João from Rio de Janeiro telling him that you had the letter, João didn't want the secret to be in danger, so he asked me to fly to Brazil to keep an eye on you. João has been a family friend since Douglas sailed to Sagres with my grandfather, Mary and I. João knows what Magellan's secret means to me, and that's why he asked me to go and meet you. My Grandpa was the one to tell Douglas about Magellan's letters. Grandpa had seen the letters in the Portuguese archive when he worked as the Harbormaster in Lisbon. When he shared with Douglas what he knew about Magellan, he didn't know that Douglas would become obsessed about it. Grandpa was just thrilled that Douglas shared the same love for navigation.

By the time João asked me to go to Brazil, you were already boarding, to Casablanca, so I flew to Morocco to meet you. João didn't want you to get lost or lose the letter since he knew how much it means to me. He convinced me to bring you to Mary's house for the night so we could come up with a plan before you went looking for him. He didn't want to tell you that he had known the truth all these years and that he had failed to tell Douglas about it. He was afraid to tell Douglas because he thought that once Douglas knew the truth, he would end his search and succumb to his disease even faster. He loved the man too much. He didn't want to see him go. When he called and I left you and Mary at the dinner table the night I brought you home, I was nervous because I didn't want to be away from the letter and you. João and I had decided that we were going to tell you the truth about everything, but when I came back home, after meeting him, I walked into the room and you were sound asleep. I took the letter from you, because I was afraid that it would get lost again. In the morning, after I left with Mary for lunch, I thought I would never see you again, but I was wrong.

When you came back to the apartment and I found you standing by the door I was completely lost, and when you saw the picture with Douglas and my family on our trip to Sagres, I didn't know what to do. The tears that I saw growing in your eyes weakened me, so I took you to João's house in Óbidos, thinking that it would be best if he told you the truth about the letters, and the reason why I didn't want the world to know about them. Then, when you saw João talking to me in the living room; you were convinced that he had betrayed you so you left us for good. I didn't run after you because I thought that I already had what I needed. I found out later that I didn't have all I needed. I was mistaken.

I have searched for you all over Brazil, but everywhere I went people denied knowing you. It was almost as if they were in compliance with you—hiding you from me, and I never thought I would be seeing you again. When you called me last week demanding the letter and the coin, I realized that it was time. I could not keep it from you any longer. You had suffered too much for it. It belonged to you.

I hope you will know what to do with it and that you will rest now. I will soon be gone, and you will reveal to the world a great secret. I hope it will give you peace, and that you will be able to move on with your life.

PS. Douglas loved you more than you will ever know.

Roland.

Chapter 55

The Coins

As I placed his letter back in the envelope, I found a key I failed to notice earlier. In the tag, there was a Lisbon address written with Roland's handwriting.

It was not over yet.

I rested with the envelope on my chest and felt the weight of the key. No. It wasn't the weight of the letter or the key that was suffocating me. It was the weight of the fear of finally learning the truth.

I tried to understand Roland's words and what it was that meant so much to him. I tried to understand why João had sent him to look after me, and I remembered Douglas telling me that if his theory was true, and Magellan had actually found the long lost continent, it would revolutionize the world of history, religion and science.

Tomorrow. Tomorrow I will find out.

I woke up with the sound of Mary knocking on my door and the smell of fresh coffee.

"Good morning," she cheered me with a smile. "Did you sleep well, honey?"

"Yes! I did."

It was true. I had slept through the entire night, which I had not done since I found out that Douglas was dead.

I drank a cup of coffee and told Mary that I had something to do in town, but not to worry because I would be back soon.

"You better!" she said smiling and I recalled the morning I had rushed out of her home before realizing that Roland had stolen the letter from me. I smiled back at her and again reassured her that I would be back.

I left the building through the iron doors that Roland had dragged me across, years ago, and waited for a cab. I gave the gentleman the address and rested, looking at Old Lisbon. In a few minutes the driver stopped in front of the building, where I walked in. The secretary, who looked fancy at the entry door, greeted me good morning and I showed her the key.

"Miss Marina?" she asked startling me.

"Yes," I answered cautiously.

She stood from the chair behind the desk and walked to the front door of the building where I had just entered. She bolted the door locked and turned back to me looking pleased.

"Follow me," she said, and walked to a set of stairs at the back of the desk.

I followed her to the underground where the cold lights shot in my eyes, making me uncertain of what to expect. Slowly, she pushed a heavy metal door open and showed me the way closing the door behind me.

The sound of the door touching the seal was sharp and fast. I looked around me and the boxes affixed into the room's walls had small doors with numbers on it. I looked for the one that matched the number on the key in my hand and placed the key in the keyhole.

I opened the metal box and I couldn't breathe. For a moment I just stood there with the box open, staring at it.

There were two coins inside it. One was the coin that Roland had stolen from me together with the letter from Magellan to his wife, and another, just the same. The coins were beautiful. They looked more like medallions. The engraving on them depicted a woman. She was standing on an island with paths guiding her all around the coin's edge. On the back there was a picture of a man. An old man.

A piece of paper beneath the coins read: Antarctica, 1989.

I placed the coins back in the safety box and went back to Mary's apartment, where I found myself alone. I prepared a bath letting the warm water run until the tub was filled enough and I let myself in, thinking about the letters.

It was all true.

Douglas trusted that Magellan had found the lost land. Douglas believed in me, and I didn't fail him.

He will finally be free.

Now that I finally had the letters and had the coins safely locked up, I just had to decide what to do with all of it.

I stayed in the tub until the water started to cool, then, I got out, wrapped my body in a towel and looked at myself in the mirror.

I left the room and called for Mary and Mena but no one answered. I wandered around the place that was so comfortable—the place where Roland had grown up—and was passing by Roland's bedroom when the bedroom door called my attention.

I opened it slowly and walked in. I scanned the whole room—the bed where Roland had slept, the dresser where he had kept his things, the walls that had seen him grow, and I approached the window to familiarize myself with his view. As I was leaving the room I was drawn to the nightstand next to his bed. Reluctantly I opened the nightstand drawer and found a picture of sunrays dancing in the sky. Roland had written: Aurora, on the back. Beneath the picture I found a small notebook. On its cover it said: 1989.

I opened the notebook and turned the pages feeling intrusive going through Roland's things, but couldn't stop myself. Some of the pages had water stains, some were ripped out and one page had a drawing of the coins I had safe in the safety box. Below the drawing it said:

"Drilling interrupted. We must save it for future generations."

I sat down on his bed and a folded piece of paper fell out of the notebook. It was a carbon copy of a letter to the Antarctica U.S. McMurdo Station authorities signed by Roland. On the letter it said that drilling had to be interrupted because of ground instability.

He had been drilling the ice, and he had found it!

Chapter 56

Into the Land

"I HAVE TO GO TO ANTARCTICA!" I told Mary when she walked in the apartment. "I have to see Roland."

Mary's eyes gleamed.

"Honey," she said, sorrowfully, "you can't get there."

"Yes I can. I need too," I told her and I started to pace back and forth on her kitchen.

Roland had found the coin and the lost land, and that's why it meant so much to him.

"If it is revealed it will change the world." He had said in the letter.

Pacing back and forth on Mary's kitchen, Roland's reasons became clear to me.

I had to see him.

I called João and told him that I finally understood. I told him that I needed help.

"Ok, Marina, I will help you," he said.

I rushed inside his shop and fell into his arms. I begged him for forgiveness. I begged him to forget that I had doubted his friendship to Douglas.

"That bastard!" He said. "He was right! The guy was

always right, and João shook his head and went to his phone where he made a call.

"Yes, yes. We can be there soon," he said on the line.

João hung up the call and grabbed his leather satchel.

"Let's go," he said, and closed the door of his atelier and we walked to his car parked down the street.

I asked him where we were going and he told me that we were going to pay a visit to an old friend—a friend from the past—a friend from when he and Douglas travelled around Europe.

The building was intimidating. The cold cement walls had no personality. One of the guards at the front gate checked our identifications and led us to the back of the building where we entered the office. A gentleman who spoke with an accent greeted us.

"João, my friend. How are you?" the man said walking toward us and shaking João's hand.

"Is this the young lady you tell me about?" he asked looking at me.

João nodded his head and looked at me confirming.

"Pleasure to meet you Sir." I told the United States ambassador to Portugal.

"The pleasure is mine, Marina."

"I am sorry to hear about Douglas," the ambassador told João honestly.

João lowered his eyes and the man continued, "Marina, you leave tomorrow to New Zealand. There are only a few flights left leaving to Antarctica. You have a couple of long days ahead of you. Are you sure you want to do this?"

I looked at João and said, "Yes, I am sure," and I saw João pleased with my answer.

*   *   *

That evening, when João and I walked out of The United States Embassy in Lisbon, João held my hand on the way to his car. Through the corner of my eyes I saw a peaceful smile on his face.

Why is he smiling?

I knew why.

Chapter 57

Antarctica

As the plane touched down on the ice, warmth filled my heart. I remembered my mother the day she found me staring at the rifle, which she had inherited from my grandmother—the one I used to kill. It was as if she knew the fate written for me. With my face between her hands, her face inches from mine, she told me: "Don't you ever, ever touch this again, do you hear me?" her eyes had a worried look in them. She relaxed her hands from my face, cautiously took the rifle from my hands and she stepped away from me. She placed the rifle again under the blankets where I had found it and closed the closet door.

I had never, ever seen my mother so mad. Seeing how mad my mom was scared me even more than finding the rifle. Before leaving the room she stopped and said, "But if you ever, ever touch it again you better know what you are doing. And if you point it at someone you better pull that trigger," she told me and walked away. We never talked about it again and I never thought about her words until the plane was touching the Antarctic ice—I had just woken up from my nightmare.

I could finally see the bullets flying from the barrel, travelling through the air, hitting my target. As I faced the hate

I knew exactly what I was doing when I pulled that trigger. I was finally free. Mom had told me what to do and I had done it.

I felt light as I walked off the plane into the sharp, freezing weather.

I was ready to face Roland.

Walking on the ice, into Roland's world, I recalled the Fortune Teller telling me my fortune.

"Ah, what nice lines!" she whispered staring at the palm of my hand, which she so gently held—a contrast from the earlier grip—as she lured me into telling my future. I wanted her to say it. Say it, and say it fast because I couldn't miss the bus going to Rio de Janeiro. I was on my way to the monastery. I was going to look for the letter Douglas told me he had seen before. I had just found out that Douglas was dead and I wanted the woman to leave me alone so I could carry on with my destiny.

"Well," she said pausing and inspecting my palm—now with very curious eyes. It was as if she had seen something so unbelievable that she had to check it twice before she told me, "Here, see? This is where everything changes." She showed me the lines on my hand, as if expecting me to confirm what she had seen. She paused again, looking in my eyes and continued, "I know it is hard to lose people you love, to lose people who loved you," and she ran a hand across her forehead, wiping the sweat that was building on it. "You are going to be fine," she said, "but not until you find the truth. Not until you understand the reasons. Only then, after you understand, you will rest," she told me. "You will have to be wise because the fate of the world will be in your hands." Slowly she let go of my hand and she walked away from me, back to her family under the tree. I ran to the bus station where I found the bus waiting— just as she told me it would be.

*   *   *

I knocked on the door of Roland's room and heard him telling me to come in. He was sitting on a chair with his back to the door and was busy writing something.

"Roland," I said.

He turned and faced me. His jaw tensed and he stared at me as if he was seeing a ghost.

"Roland," I said again, and stepped inside the room.

Roland stood from the small chair, making me again aware of his demeanor. He ran his hand through his hair, looked around the room as if looking for something, then cleaned a space on his bed and offered me a place to sit down.

"I am sorry." I said. "I am sorry for showing up like this," and I sat on the bed.

Roland sat back down on the small chair by the desk, crossed his leg and faced me.

"I am sorry," he told me, lowering his eyes.

"I am sorry for what I've done to you. You didn't deserve it."

"No, I didn't." I said. "I didn't deserve much that had happened to me, but it happened and I survived," I told him coldly.

Roland walked toward me and took my hands. This time I stood without propping myself. There was no airline counter for me to lean on, no cold wall to hold my back against, but I stood still. My heart raced in my chest, my knees threatened to fail me, but I didn't let Roland stop anymore. I was there to tell him that his secret was safe with me. To tell him that now that I knew the truth, the search was done and that there was nothing to be revealed—not in our lifetime, and I told him. I told him everything I had traveled so far away to tell him.

We sat in his room in silence—a silence that didn't need to be broken.

Roland walked me out of his room and out of the station to where the cold sun was still lighting the day. He drove me to an even more remote area where we stood facing the glaciers, which were balancing on the cold ocean. Behind us, the icy mountains remained untouched—protected. Land put his arm on my shoulder and I cuddled under it. He touched my face with his gloved hand and kissed my lips with his broken lips. We stared in each other's eyes, aware of the secret that was safe between us and we drove back to the station.

The End

IT WAS THE LAST RAYS OF SUN I was going to see in the next six months. I took a deep breath and stepped inside. Roland closed the door behind us, leaving to the world, the wonders, and the tempests which that land still has to fight in order for one day to rise again. Only then, its debilitation will be forgiven and the world, which once was, will rise again.

After All

"JEAN! YOU LOOK AMAZING!" I told him falling into his arms.

Behind him, Ramón was all jealous, rolling his eyes.

"You look good too!" I told him as he embraced my shoulder under his arm taking me away from Jean.

They did look great. Retirement was treating them well. They seemed happy and the tan on their skin was making them radiant.

"I can't believe you are here, cherie" Jean said vibrant.

I spent a week in Jean and Ramón's apartment in Biarritz. It felt invigorating. Carla flew in from London, where she has been living with some British boyfriend, and she told me that her cousin Luis was still the same—a gallant!

Elisa came from Italy by herself, where she left her young family behind. She indeed found a hot Italian, with whom she had a beautiful daughter and is happily married.

It was an amazing weekend, we shared our new lives and we laughed, recalling the good times onboard the *Queen Leonor*, but when we said goodbye we didn't know when we were going to see each other again.

From there I took a train to Cádiz, where I went to visit my friends at *Casa Blanca*.

Señor Antúnez was waiting for me. It was as if he knew what I was there to do. We sat on the veranda facing their sea and I showed him the letter, then he turned it around and saw the map—the map, which he had seen in Jaime's ship. He took a deep breath and I placed one coin in his hand. He stared at it for a moment and faced the horizon, where I am sure he saw the spirit of Jaime vanishing away.

Now he will rest.

I walked out of the *Casa Blanca* and went to the harbor where Rafael was waiting for me on board the *True North*. I boarded the vessel, and the sail unfurled and gently the wind blew us away.

Roland would wait for me, while Rafael was going to show me what Douglas felt, sailing the waters that carried our explorers to unknown worlds.

Acknowledgements

DYLAN, I would not have done it without you.

I want to thank Vera, for loving my story and treating it as if it was her own. I want to thank Kate, my stone keeper, for encouraging me. I want to thank João, for teaching me about sailing on the coast of Portugal. I want to thank Ryan, for telling me how to get to the bottom of the world. I want to thank Su and Todd, for teaching me where to tie my boat, Maria, for living the first chapters, and Brigitta, for walking on the sidewalk. I want to thank Sara, for giving me punch and I want to thank Shelly, Dulce, Elaine and Monique for reading with open eyes. I want to thank my book club girls; Tina, Jen, Liz, Heidi, Lynn, Christy, Heather, Lauren and Jacqueline, for listening to me throughout my blabbering. I want to thank Jamie, for accepting the voice, Laura, for sharing her knowledge, Diane, for cooking me dinner, and Mark, for pushing me forward. I want to thank Michal, for the electrifying cover art, and Eric, for the clever book layout. And last, but not least, I want to thank Minha Mãe, and Meu Irmão, for being there.

About the Author

I GREW UP IN BRAZIL, but left when I was twenty years old. My life could have gone bad, but somehow, thanks to a God I believe exists, and, as some say, to my intuition, things aligned and my way was always clear. At times, life carried me in its arms, and at others, I walked with my own feet. Like a friend of mine used to say, "I was born with my ass towards the moon." I still don't know if it is true, but perhaps, she may be right—because of all of the times I was carried through. Today, I have all I always dreamed of but I haven't stopped dreaming. I live in a house by the sea, I have a beautiful daughter who keeps me busy, and a husband, a horse, a dog and two cats that keep me even busier. The Thief of Secrets is my first novel and I wrote it on my kitchen desk. I hope you loved reading it, as much I loved writing it.